DECEPTION

Book 1.5 in the *Divided* series

CC ROBINSON

Manifold Publishing
Cincinnati

Published in the United States by Manifold Publishing, LLC, Cincinnati, OH.

Identifiers: ISBN 978-1-962912-05-1 (pbk.) | ISBN 978-1-962912-04-4 (ebook)

Cover Design by 100 Covers.

To Ruth, my Oxford-comma finder extraordinaire.
What would I do without you?
Destroy grammar, that's what!

CC ROBINSON

1

Sophie replaced the lock picking set in her right jacket packet and opened the door into Hudson Britwell's office. The key opposition leader kept his office neat as a pin, but Sophie knew where he kept the interesting documents. She'd been searching it regularly for years, delving into paperwork and hidden drawer bottoms to unearth the opposition's schemes before they destroyed the city. And also to ensure Britwell knew nothing of her beloved Underground movement.

Closing his door behind her, she clicked on the small penlight and bee-lined for his large maple desk. Such expense and waste, but the commissioned piece told her where Britwell kept his secrets. Only a handcrafted original like this would have false drawer bottoms and hidden latches.

Opening the large bottom drawer, Sophie removed the stack of rations paperwork and market inventories, setting them gently on the floor at her feet.

She couldn't risk moving anything on top of the desk even an inch. Britwell would notice and know for sure someone spied on him. Which would only make him more dangerous than he already was. A politician with an insatiable thirst for power, Britwell was on the brink of forcing Sophie's boss, Mayor Kim, out of his position. If they allowed Britwell to win, they'd compromise everything Kim and their alliance around the city had worked for — equity in rations and market item availability, more spots in the Queenstown College admin track for students not related to or selected by the city's power brokers, and fairer trials for imprisoned citizens in the Central Prison.

Life in the Federated Republic of America was hard, and they could only do so much. But Kim and his allies had worked hard for these basic improvements, and Sophie wouldn't allow that progress to evaporate in one fell swoop. She wished they could dismantle the walls dividing their city into ethnic areas, or free up commerce, but those felt like impossible wishes after more than four decades of Martin's iron-fisted rule over the FRA.

She pressed the hidden latch, releasing the locking mechanism and opening the false drawer bottom. He thought himself so clever, but little did Britwell know that this was as basic a hidden space as Sophie had ever seen. Her own hiding space in her closet floor was far more complex. Sophie lifted the first few files, stacking them horizontally on the pile.

Nothing new.

Her mouth dropped open at the paper that lay halfway down. Requisition orders that made her heart drop into her toes. Patrol-issued rifles, army-issued Chinese-made revolvers and ammunition, and uniforms. Hundreds of uniforms. In all sizes, but every last one black with no blazing patrols emblem for the left breast.

As the kids these days said, "What in Martin's macrocosm?"

She thumbed through the remaining files.

More of the same.

She'd last been in this office a few months ago, and now Britwell had all these weapons? And ammunition, uniforms, boots, rations bars, and, of all things, canned goods. What was he up to? And where was all this loot?

Sophie had replaced the last file into the drawer and was exiting Britwell's office when footsteps thundered up the marble staircase which wound up the front of the Central Administrative Building, or the CAB, as everyone called it. She glanced toward the rear stairwell and quickly realized she would never make it, even running at a sprint.

The janitor's closet beckoned to her, and Sophie ducked inside. She clicked her flashlight off as voices echoed through the third-floor hallway housing the Ivory area delegation. Her own Little Asian area offices were on the floor below, along with the Havana area offices. Obsidian offices shared the ground floor with the towering lobby, marble staircase, and the city council conference room with its over-sized mahogany table.

Sophie held her breath when the footsteps stopped. The jingle of keys filled the air.

"Come on in," Hudson Britwell's distinctive gruff voice said to whoever was with him.

"Hud, we need to talk about where you're storing everything," the clipped accent betrayed the woman's Gateway City roots, but who was this?

"Madam Secretary," Hudson said, "I am not so naïve as you think. Of course I've worked out where to store everything. And yes, recruitment is going as planned, before you ask about that."

The Secretary of State?

Why was Gonzalez here? It had to be her. She was the only female cabinet secretary from Gateway City.

Sophie suspected there was more to that woman than met the eye. Anyone who could maneuver onto Supreme Commander Martin's cabinet deserved respect as a cold-hearted political strategist. Add in that she was from Gateway City and not Martinsburg, and Sophie's suspicions grew wings.

"Good," that was a much younger voice. The man couldn't be more than thirty years old. He continued, "we don't have much time left. Your role in this plan is small but critical, my friend. If we don't succeed here, the next phase is questionable, as are our lives."

In her many years of spying, Sophie had learned to distinguish certain characteristics just from a person's voice. The timbre, tone, warbles, wavers, hints of accents, and so on.

The young man had spent time in both Ivory and Havana, though most listeners wouldn't pick up on his Havana accent. It was barely there, in the cadence of his sentences and in how he'd said "my friend." That wasn't an Ivory saying. Havanas tagged on "mi amigo" to everything. Had the man picked that habit up, only using English instead of Nuevo Havana? Or was this his attempt to mask his ethnic roots? Something to ponder later.

"Our allies are getting antsy," Gonzalez said. "They want their hands on the weapon yesterday."

Allies.

That implied conspiracy with an enemy of the Federated Republic of America. The FRA allied with China, United Korea, Cuba, and Russia. Its enemies were practically the rest of the civilized world, the nations who'd survived the world war sparked by America's last Great Civil War. It could be absolutely anyone wanting "the weapon."

And a weapon? What weapon? Was this the program Rose had insisted on applying for? The one Sophie doubted was only studying nuclear power, satellites, and space?

Martin couldn't have sophisticated weaponry, especially not nuclear weapons. International treaties forbade it after the fragile peace with the Independent Republic of Texas and Canada. That peace had been in place forty-plus years, negotiated after those nations tried to assassinate the newly self-appointed Supreme Commander Martin. Obviously, they'd failed.

Sophie and Rose had argued many times about Rose's stubborn insistence on applying for the elite physicist training program. Before Sophie had snuck out and into central for what was supposed to be a routine, and short, spy errand, they'd argued again. If her daughter was accepted to the program, there'd be added scrutiny on their household.

Sophie could kiss these nighttime errands goodbye. Along with most of her other Underground duties.

Why Rose refused to listen to Sophie's best arguments was beyond her. Of course, Sophie had mentioned nothing about her spy work or the Underground. That would've been stupid to trust Rose with those secrets. Her daughter had buried her head inside textbooks most of her life. Secrets weren't something Rose could be trusted with.

Sophie nearly growled in frustration at the picture coming into focus, but held it in, not wanting to alert the others to her presence.

Britwell was amassing supplies for an army.

Gonzalez and someone else were scheming with unnamed allies to steal a weapon Martin secretly possessed.

But why? What was their end goal?

She wanted to know - no, needed to know - all of this. Lives were at stake.

Sophie shuffled her numb feet, wiggling her toes, hitting something hanging on the wall. A wooden handled mop clattered off the wall behind her, knocking into her head, the mop threads tangling in her feet. She froze.

"What was that?" Gonzalez said.

"I'll investigate," Britwell said, his chair colliding with the wooden credenza behind his desk.

Sophie threw open the closet door and bolted toward the rear staircase.

"Hey, you!" Britwell's voice boomed through the hallway. "Stop right where you are, traitor!"

She slammed the heavy steel door open and vaulted down the stairs, taking them three or four at a time and throwing herself around the corners of the landings. Footsteps scrambled after her and a gunshot rang out. She ducked away from the center of the staircase and quickened her descent.

"Don't think I won't catch you," the man with the Ivory-Havana accent yelled.

He fired again. The bullet bounced off the stairwell and embedded into the wall behind her. That was too close.

Where was Cletus?

The gunshots should've drawn the night security guard like a fly to day-old stir-fry.

When she reached the ground floor, Sophie threw open the metal emergency exit door and the door alarm blared through the night. She dodged around the side of the CAB and sprinted toward Little Asia.

When she had emerged from the alleyway between the CAB and its neighbor, an empty warehouse, the same emergency exit door slammed open.

Sophie had maybe ten seconds' lead on the younger man. He'd catch her, if only because of his youth. It had been decades since she'd beaten the younger men in the Underground at their tunnel sprint races, despite her frequent training.

A white van idled in front of the CAB. Sophie ran past it and down another alleyway.

She tossed a wave to the man guarding the loading dock of the warehouse across from the CAB. She'd grown accustomed to their presence, though every inquiry she or Mr. Kim made into what they were guarding had hit a brick wall of silence. It was "Martin regime business," or so they were told.

Sophie kept to the alleyways, sprinting between the empty warehouses and buildings of Central, terror filling her throat. The gate into Little Asia came into view as the same white van shrieked around a corner several blocks to the east.

It was a race to the gate.

The Little Asian gate guard, a young man named Chul, whom her daughter had tutored, saw her and opened the sally port door. His eyes widened, and he gestured wildly for her to hurry.

Sophie sprinted toward him, still fifty yards away. The van sped through the silent intersection, eating up another block with a squeal of tires.

A metal glint caught her eye.

Sophie wove as she ran, bullets chewing up the pavement feet away from where she sprinted. Rocks pinged her legs, sending darts of pain through her body. Chul stepped out of the gate and returned fire.

"Cover me, Matsuko!"

The middle-aged patrol officer hid behind the metal gate and fired at the now-slowing van. A tire exploded, and the van spun out of control, heading straight for a light pole across from the gate.

Chul stepped in front of Sophie as she finally reached the gate, firing shot after shot at the driver. The man ducked, but not before Chul's bullets crashed through the driver's side window and found his shoulder. His screams of agony and the other man's shouts to return fire and move the van mingled, increasing Sophie's terror.

"Get in!" Matsuko shoved Sophie through the sally port gate, while Chul radioed for backup. They locked the gate, sealing the white van and its inhabitants out of Little Asia. Sirens filled the air.

"Get out of here to someplace safe," Chul said, raising his eyebrows.

She knew where he hinted for her to go, yet everything inside her resisted. Sophie wanted to see those men arrested, tortured for their information, giving up the powerful Britwell in the process and taking down his entire operation.

"You need to leave unless you want to be taken into custody," Matsuko said.

"We'll cover for you," Chul added. "Since Mr. Kim sent you on your errand. But our captain will want to know who chased you and why they tried to kill you."

Sophie didn't trust the Little Asian captain. Something fishy was going on in Little Asian patrols, and she wasn't talking about the captain's love of sardines. He'd never believe her story about Britwell. Sophie suspected Captain Romel owed Britwell for his kid's college slot.

She growled in frustration. "I hate this so much. But you're right," Sophie threw a goodbye wave over her shoulder and disappeared into the shadows of Tower Four.

Before the patrol's hovercycles had reached the gate area, she had entered the locked emergency exit. Silence and the stairwell's bright fluorescent light greeted her. She sprinted down the stairs to the basement level and exited to the dim hallway leading to the mechanical room and the Underground entrance.

Sophie opened the mechanical room door and the concealed underground tunnel entrance by rote memory alone, her brain circling around who the young man was and what they were all up to. Resting her head against the tunnel's cool cement wall, Sophie breathed deeply in and out. She'd made it. Somehow she'd survived.

But now she couldn't go back to her life. And Rose would have to understand, even though she'd never get an explanation.

***

Sophie had missed her daughter's big moment in the spotlight.

Rose had appeared on the evening broadcast, accepting her slot in Martin's illustrious nuclear physicist training program.

And no one had batted an eye.

Not her boss.

Not the other Underground members who'd shown up after the mandatory announcement to train or workout at HQ.

And now Sophie stood across from the man everyone else called Tío, or Alejandro to her, whose scowl and posture screamed his anger at her.

"I told her to not go through with it," Sophie said, pacing between the sink and the wall in the small kitchen inside HQ. She'd been stuck here for a day and already she was about to go insane. "I told her Martin couldn't have nuclear weapons, so this had to be something bad. Something that would land us all in trouble with the international community. But, no. She defies me and does it anyway."

"She's grown now. Graduated from high school," said Alejandro. "You have to let her make her own decisions."

Sophie growled and leaned into the kitchen table across from where he stood. "She wouldn't listen to me."

"And you're not listening to me."

"How dare she do this? It puts everything we've worked for at risk. And for what? For more textbooks? More learning?"

"Do you not see? You've lived with your daughter for eighteen years now, but do you really know her, Sophie?"

Sophie turned her back to him and folded her arms over her chest.

"Remember back when we met?" he asked.

How could she forget? He was a dashing driver recruit, full of himself and his fighting abilities.

They met first in the Little Asian depot where he caught her eye. But she ignored him and his antics, his too-big personality. Until they'd met again at HQ.

"You were running that place. So bossy. So sure of yourself."

Sophie snorted out a laugh. "Running the place? I was a secretary, Alejandro. Secretaries don't run anything."

He walked around the table to face her, dropping a hand to her shoulder. "And yet, you ran that place. The admin was never around. Never bothered to come in. You knew what you could do and you did it. Unashamedly, without hesitation. Maybe your daughter isn't so different from you, after all? She simply has different interests."

"She's going to get herself and the rest of us killed."

"Did you ever tell her about the Underground? Invite her in?" He ducked his head to connect gazes until Sophie lowered her eyes to his chest. For a forty-five year old, he was still built like the side of a house.

Sophie shook her head and pushed past him. "I've told you a million times, she's not fit for our movement. She can't keep secrets, can't sneak around, and definitely can't lie. She would tell a patrol officer everything if it meant one more day of learning. Her priorities aren't the same as mine. As ours."

"Are you sure about that? Didn't you complain about how she's constantly wanting to touch the wall?"

She waved her hand in the air. "That's because of the tech, not because she hates being trapped inside them."

"Are you positive? Have you asked her? Have you ever talked about why she wants to do this program? She looked so excited on the announcement last night, Sophie."

"So I heard. Maybe she was just excited I disappeared."

"Disappeared? What are you talking about?"

"I had to flee two nights ago. Left with only the clothes on my back. I barely escaped into the tunnels before the Little Asian captain detained me."

"What did you do this time?" Alejandro cradled his head in his palm.

"Not me. Hudson Britwell."

She was pacing again, trying to work out how to stop the madman on the city council from accumulating power and destroying everything they'd worked for. Never mind Rose. Britwell was the far greater threat.

Alejandro grabbed her by the upper arms and turned her to face him. "Please, you're making me dizzy with all this pacing."

She relaxed in his grip. Maybe together they could figure this out. "I was doing my normal surveillance and spy time in Britwell's office, checking his not-so-secret drawer for anything new and I hit the motherlode. He's amassing guns, ammo, patrol uniforms that aren't emblazoned with the patrol emblem, boots, rations, and, strangely enough, canned goods. Like he's building an army base outside of the city's distro system."

"What?"

"It can't be anything less than a power grab," Sophie said, her gaze on Alejandro's. She desperately needed him to see what was so obvious to her. "Think about it. Guns and ammo because they need a way to seize power. Food because his recruits will use it to bribe the gate guards to leave the city to train and plan. Then they'd need patrol uniforms so no one inside the city suspects a thing until they've already taken over."

Alejandro stroked his mustache. She remained silent, allowing him to process everything. "You need to bring Rose into the Underground, Sophie," he said.

Her eyes widened. That's the conclusion he came to? She tells him Hudson Britwell is assembling a militia at best, an army at worse, and no one knows why — and that's what he wants to do? That's his best next action?

She ripped away from him and stomped out of the kitchen.

"Sophie," he yelled, running into the hallway after her. He finally caught her right before she entered the training room, the loud bass of a song from the early 2000s blaring from the music system.

"Can't you see?" He blocked her path.

She didn't mind his involvement. Not really. She just wished he'd see her perspective.

"Rose is a sitting duck now that you're not around. She needs to know the truth so she can protect herself and you. You can't go back to life as normal in Little Asia, Sophie. But if she thinks you just abandoned her, then when — not if — someone comes asking questions about you, she won't know how to cover for you. She could ruin everything with conjecture and half-truths."

"What if I don't want to tell her everything? And would she believe me anyway? She fights me on everything I say."

"I'll go with you," Alejandro said. "She has no reason to not trust me — at least not yet. And with someone new around, she's less likely to lash out at you."

Sophie's shoulders deflated. Maybe he was right and she should've told Rose about the Underground and her role in it a long time ago.

But he was wrong about one thing — Sophie's relationship with Rose was beyond salvageable. Her daughter hated her, and with good reason. Sophie had kept Rose at arms' length for well over a decade, ever since Rose started burying her nose in textbooks. Secrets stayed that way when the fewest possible number of people knew them.

2

S ophie led Alejandro out of the stairwell of her tower in Little Asia, a finger on her lips. Of course, he knew to stay quiet. Maybe he was onto something with her always needing to control others. But that was something she'd examine later. Much later.

Sophie removed her key, opening the front door of her condo. She'd oiled the hinges recently, and was now thankful for her own foresight. No squeaking to awaken the neighbors, especially the pesky one across the hall. Sophie closed the door behind them, bustling around the room to catalog the listening devices. She sighed out.

"No new ones," Sophie said.

Alejandro's eyes widened, and he motioned a zipping of his lips.

"I've disabled them, and Rose would've found and disabled any new ones."

"You taught her how to disable listening devices but she doesn't know about the Underground? Sophie..." he whispered before sinking into their threadbare couch, the only one they could afford.

"What's going on?" Rose asked. She wore her favorite sweatshirt and jeans, her sneakers already on and laced up.

"Have you disabled any new listening devices?" Sophie asked, scanning the room for the usual patrol hiding places.

"As far as I know, yes." Rose rubbed the sleep from her eyes. "Where have you been? And who are you?" She pointed to Alejandro.

"Something happened."

"What?" Rose crossed her arms over her chest and cocked a hip out.

Sophie recognized the stubborn set to her daughter's jaw. This wouldn't go well.

"I've been in hiding."

"What in Martin's macrocosm?" Rose cursed, making Sophie flinch. "And you didn't answer my question," she said as she pointed at Alejandro with her eyebrows raised.

"Let's head to the roof," Sophie whispered as she passed Rose. "There's a lot you don't know."

"You can say that again," said Rose.

Sophie allowed Rose to lead, gesturing for Alejandro to precede her as she locked the door behind them. She'd seen Rose upset, but this was another level. Sophie's stomach filled with dread and her feet dragged up the rear staircase.

They exited to the tower's snowy rooftop, and Sophie closed the access door behind them. Alejandro led Rose by the elbow to the low mechanical building, where they could sit sheltered away from the blistery wind. Late winter was unpredictable, and this year had brought a rare March snow storm to Queenstown. It'd melt in a day or two, but Sophie wouldn't be around to see it.

They sat in a row on the gravel against the mechanical building, the chilly predawn darkness making Sophie wish she had her winter coat. But it had been warmer the day she'd fled, so she hadn't worn a coat. She'd have to grab more winter clothing before returning to HQ.

Rose stared at the gravel.

Steeling herself with a deep breath, Sophie said, "There's so much you don't know."

Rose opened her mouth, but Alejandro's hand on Rose's forearm made her snap it closed. "Your mother is only trying to protect you.

But she's in trouble, and you could be in danger, too. I think it's about time you knew the truth."

"Who are you to know anything about me?"

Oh boy. How did Sophie answer this question without giving everything away? "Let me start at the beginning," Sophie said. "This is Tío, or Uncle in Nuevo Havana. His real name isn't important. But before we explain who he is and why he's here, you need to know some history. Before Martin unified the nation, there was the Great Civil War, which I know you know about."

Rose started to say something, but Alejandro once again stopped her.

Sophie barreled on. "Right before the FRA formed, city leaders here assembled a militia from the various ethnic groups who had once been fighting each other. But it was too-little-too-late. Martin defeated them and shoved everyone into the city. Most militia members hid in plain sight inside Queenstown's four areas. Instead of letting Martin do what he wanted, they started a rebel organization that still exists today."

Rose's eyes widened and Sophie watched her daughter connect the dots. She knew Rose had arrived at the truth when her daughter's nostrils flared, her jaw tensed, and she bunched up the fabric of her sweatshirt in a tight fist.

"Tío and I met in that organization. It's called the Underground."

"We aim to bring down the Martin regime and reunite the nation," Tío said.

Rose leaned forward, a thousand questions written all over her face.

He extended his palm toward Rose, and Sophie continued.

"No more walls. No more division. It's been slow work, though. We met decades ago at our headquarters, in tunnels underneath the city — thus the name. That's where I've been hiding, by the way."

Sophie patted Rose's knee, then withdrew her hand as if a snake had bitten it. Her mother, Rose's Grandma Angie, had been the touchy person in the family. Since her death Sophie and Rose rarely touched. Now touching her own grown daughter felt weird.

The silence went on and on, and Sophie waited.

Would Rose love all this, or would she explode in anger? Sophie cataloged the emotions flashing across her daughter's face, and marveled at the breadth. Sophie rarely felt any emotion, and when she did, she struggled to contain it.

Rose darted to her feet. "How could you do this to me?"

Sophie winced at Rose's yell, and Rose clamped a hand over her own mouth. At least Rose was aware of her surroundings for once.

Sophie schooled her breathing so she didn't yell back at her daughter. "How many times have I had to stop you from touching — actually touching! — the wall?" Sophie asked. "Clearly you're curious about the other areas. You should be thanking me for this opportunity." She was impressed she'd sounded so calm, so unaffected, when Sophie really wanted to give Rose back what she'd gotten — rage and anger.

"Opportunity? So far I hear nothing about an 'opportunity.' I have a fantastic opportunity and you didn't want me to pursue it. Said I should withdraw my name." Rose paced the roof.

And Sophie had been right. The program was dangerous, and would place Rose far too close to regime power brokers for Sophie's comfort. Part of how Sophie had remained free was by not flying too close to the sun of power.

"And, besides, every time I reached toward the wall or pondered aloud about the other areas, you told me we had to obey Martin, follow his rules, not rock the boat so you wouldn't lose your precious job. I was doing fine without you!"

Sophie dipped her chin. All of that was the safe way to exist under the dictatorship, to live and not be executed for treason. Of course, Sophie had taught Rose to walk the line.

"In case you hadn't heard, I got into the physicist program — like you even care — and will be working on important projects. The only thing I ever wanted was to be accepted for who I am and that's finally happening. I'll get to work with people from other areas. But now you tell me you want all that to end?" Rose said, her finger pointed at Sophie's chest.

"How much of your life was a lie? Are you even telling me the truth now?"

Sophie felt Rose's accusation like a punch, reeling backward, her head bouncing against the brick wall behind her. Rose had everything so twisted up. Sophie didn't want to keep Rose out of the program for any reason other than her daughter's safety. She hadn't told Rose about the Underground in order to protect her. Sophie was the only one around to protect them. So she had been both mother and father. Nurturer and protector. Why couldn't Rose see and appreciate all she'd done?

Rose snorted. "What about all those meetings I couldn't be in? Or the times you and Carrie Wang went off somewhere and left me at the Kims' condo for hours?"

Which was a perfectly acceptable and safe place for her to be. Mrs. Kim was a lovely person. She wouldn't hurt a fly. And Rose couldn't be around while she'd taught the older Carrie Wang how to pick locks, avoid cameras, and sneak into and out of public places like the Market or the Distro. Secrecy for those training sessions had ensured Carrie could accomplish her role.

"You didn't want me involved," Rose said. She sank back to sit against the wall, as if her anger had deflated.

Sophie knew better, though.

"You wanted me ignorant and left out. 'Just study, Rose,' 'Don't ask questions, Rose.' Why tell me all this now?"

Sophie shot to her feet and stalked over to Rose on Alejandro's other side. She leaned in close so she wouldn't need to yell. "I was trying to protect you."

Rose turned a shoulder away.

"Let's calm down," Tío said, his hands extended to them both. "Your mother made a mistake by not telling you this earlier."

Sophie opened her mouth to protest, but Alejandro raised a palm.

"No, Sophie. You should've told Rose everything a long time ago. This," he gestured between them, "would be in much better shape if you had. But we can't go back in time."

Sophie crossed her arms over her chest and clamped her jaw shut. How dare he insert himself into Rose's life now, when Sophie had to remain at HQ, in hiding.

Rose huffed. "Clearly you're still involved in this Underground," Rose said. "Why do you work for the mayor? Why implement Martin's policies if you're this big rebel? And how did you sneak him into our condo?" Rose rolled her eyes as if she wouldn't believe anything Sophie said. And she probably wouldn't.

Sophie hung her head, exhaustion filling her core. "One question at a time. I promise I'll answer," her mother replied.

She nodded to Alejandro and steeled herself for Rose's anger explosion. "I'm a spy in the city council."

"Ok. So, you're a spy. That still doesn't explain why you opposed me going for the program?"

"Britwell saw me..." Sophie cut off her own words.

"Sophie," said Tío.

"Not going there," she said. Sophie had many reasons she'd opposed Rose's application to Martin's fancy nuclear physics doctorate. The program was a sham, meant to hide what was really happening in the capital. And Sophie was determined to figure it out.

"This is so counter," Rose pointed to Alejandro. Sophie could hardly keep up with the slang Rose threw about. But, this one she knew.

"But necessary. I'd love for you to come with me to our headquarters. It's underground, outside the city. You'll get to meet young men and women your age from the other areas," Alejandro said.

How dare he just blurt that out. She'd decided to tell Rose about the Underground, not bring her in as an operative. Sophie closed her eyes and tilted her head back. How could she salvage this disaster?

Rose peppered them with questions — about Sophie's exact role, the Kims' status as operatives or not, and why Sophie was in hiding. Of course, neither she nor Alejandro answered any of Rose's questions directly. Let the girl sit on the truth she'd learned before they trusted her with more.

"Fine," Rose finally relented.

Sophie nearly wept with relief. Her daughter seriously could be an interrogator.

"Ok. I want in. Starting today. I'm behind. You know I can fight, of course. We learn jujitsu in PE."

Sophie exchanged a glance with Alejandro, hers more of a glare. He shrugged his massive shoulders with a smile. Mark one point for Alejandro, none for Sophie.

"We'll take you to our headquarters today," Sophie said. "But Rose, you must guard these secrets with your life." Sophie pushed up her sweatshirt sleeve and scratched at a bug bite on her forearm, wondering how she'd gotten it since it was still cold and dreary in Queenstown. Probably a spider bite.

"And about that program..." Sophie said.

Alejandro cut her off. She was ready to punch him for interfering. "You need to do it, Rose."

"Of course. That was my plan."

Sophie huffed and shook her head. She'd lost all control of the conversation. Now Rose would see where Sophie had been hiding for the last few days. She'd know all of Sophie's secrets. Well, not all. But too many for Sophie's liking.

Rose vaulted to her feet and Alejandro stood, drawing Sophie up beside him. Her knees cracked as usual, and she smiled at Alejandro in thanks.

Rose gazed at them, a wrinkle forming between her eyebrows. Tío squeezed Rose's shoulders and pivoted her toward the stairs.

Sophie couldn't handle any more questions today. She was maxed out on revealing secrets. Sophie trailed behind them as they descended the rear staircase.

They stopped off briefly at their floor, and Sophie ran to grab a few winter clothing items. When she returned, Alejandro still peppered Rose with questions about the program. Rose explained the study of physics in space and the physical nature of stars.

Sophie zoned them out. When they reached the first level, Sophie interrupted Rose's explanation of telescopes both on the ground and in orbit and why they needed both.

"Time for quiet," she said.

Sophie checked the back hallway leading to their tower's mechanical room and the closest entrance to the secret tunnel system beneath Queenstown. Never before had Sophie been so thankful for this resource. When they reached the bottom of the steep metal staircase into the tunnels, Rose stopped and stared at the walls and the fluorescent lighting along the ceiling. Rose laughed, dropping her hands to her knees.

"Wow. This is... just wow. How did these tunnels get here? Does Martin know we're using his electricity? And why wasn't there a camera in that hallway?"

"So many questions," Alejandro said.

Maybe he was tiring of her daughter's constant questions, too. But it was too late to take Rose back to the condo. They were committed.

"My mother used the tunnels before the Civil War and found the entrances once Queenstown was walled in," Alejandro said. "We made some improvements. And no, Martin doesn't know we siphon electricity. It's hidden as a draw from the factories." He headed toward their left at a jog. "Let's go."

"And there's never been a camera in that hallway, only the lobby," she added, pumping her arms to catch up to Alejandro's long-legged pace. "And so far I don't think the regime realizes this. Let's not tip them off, okay?"

Rose nodded as she jogged next to her, not even out of breath. Maybe her PE training was better than Sophie realized.

"So, what will I do today?" Rose asked.

"You'll start on the firing range," she said.

"Or maybe in basic self-defense," Alejandro interjected. "Even with your PE jujitsu units, I doubt you're ready to spar with an Underground operative."

"Ok," Rose said. "What's a 'firing range'?"

Tío chuckled, lengthening his stride. Both Sophie and Rose pumped their arms to keep up. Show off.

"You'll see soon enough," he said.

And Sophie would attempt to limit how many secrets Rose found out in one day, but knowing Alejandro, he'd lay everything at one smile from her daughter. He'd turned into a softie in his middle years.

3

Sophie hadn't forgotten that Alejandro had blown off her intel about Hudson Britwell amassing an army. Maybe he didn't believe her. Or maybe it terrified him to confront the truth.

It scared her to pieces, too, but she'd gain nothing by ignoring reality. Sophie realized she needed independent verification. She'd hate it if Britwell was lying through his teeth about everything, just to impress some Martin cabinet members and vault himself into power.

So, she sought the one person who would know — and who'd tell her — the truth.

Sophie mounted the stairs into Tower One, her boss's residential tower, pausing at the door into the mechanical room.

No need to walk in on some repairman and reveal the underground tunnel entrance.

Hearing nothing but the hum of the furnace, Sophie opened the heavy metal door and entered the darkened mechanical room. She made quick work of locking the metal door, replacing the concealing panel, and exiting the mechanical room into the dim — and camera-less — basement hallway.

It was a rarity to be somewhere in the FRA without the watchful eyes of the regime on you.

Sophie donned her knit cap, pulling it low over her eyes, and raised her coat collar against her face. She couldn't risk being recognized, but she had no choice except to travel the streets of Little Asia, still decorated for the New Year celebration with festive lanterns, to Tower Two, where her contact lived. Hopefully, she'd be home.

Sophie stepped out of the tower, the streetlights already on as the sun descended toward the horizon. Long shadows draped the area in intermittent darkness, broken by the cool orange glow of a late winter sunset. She kept her chin tucked into her coat and her hands in her pockets, looking as if she were both in a hurry and extremely cold. Good thing most people out this close to curfew didn't bother exchanging the lengthy Little Asian greetings — smiles, bows, and pleasantries about families and work.

She rushed across Main Street and past the first floor lobby of Tower Two, ducking into the alleyway between Towers Two and Three. The guard on lobby duty would know her in an instant, and there went her freedom. He'd call the patrols captain, and she'd be in lockup.

Sophie palmed her key to the emergency exit door. Once she reached the door, she worked fast, unlocking, opening, and locking the door, then punching in the disarm code only patrols and the fire teams knew. Or rather, supposedly knew. At some point, they'd check the camera feed and realize the person who'd disarmed the door was both small and concealing their identity. But by then, Sophie would be long gone.

She darted up the stairwell, pumping her arms and taking the steps two at a time to the fourth floor. Sprinting, she screeched to a halt outside the Wang apartment. The door opened almost immediately at her short coded knock. Carrie's eyes widened, then she looked up and down the hallway before dragging Sophie into her apartment by the wrist.

"What are you doing here?" Carrie asked. "I heard you had to run."

"I did," Sophie said. "I need you to check into something for me. But I have to make this quick. I tripped the emergency exit alarm downstairs."

Carrie smacked a palm to her knee. "Not again. Ok. What's up?"

"Have canned goods and rations bars gone missing? Any strange shipments into Central that then disappear into thin air?"

"Yes and no," Carrie said. "Yes, pallets of canned goods, rations bars, and cigarettes have gone missing lately. Over the last...um...maybe six weeks?"

"Cigarettes, too? That's the perfect bribery for a gate guard." Sophie paced the small living room, avoiding the scratched wood table set into the center and Carrie's position next to the door.

"And not really about the shipments. Junior — I only know who that is from that announcement and, by the way, congratulations on Rose's acceptance to the program, you must be so proud. Anyway, Junior unloaded pallet after pallet from his yacht. Hudson Britwell was there too, directing a group of men to transfer everything into trucks. It was at night and they knocked the Central Depot guard out, but they didn't know I saw the whole thing. Something about Junior's yacht bothered me when he docked that day, so I hid. I was going to board the yacht and investigate when the moving-stolen-goods party started. Didn't get a look at the box labels, but they seemed heavy by how the men grunted while moving it all."

"Then it's true. He's really doing this."

"Doing what?"

"Britwell is amassing a militia. I don't know where or why. Except that's not true. He wants to take over Queenstown. And maybe there's more. Junior said something about allies. Maybe they want to depose Martin, which would be my guess, but will they be any better? Doubtful."

"Let me in. I'll infiltrate this militia. Get close to Junior."

"It's too dangerous."

"Who else is there? You know I'm the only one trained for this role. I'm the right age, too."

"I don't like it," Sophie said, hands on her hips as she glared at Carrie, who was like a second daughter to her. Sophie knew why Carrie wanted in on this. She wanted revenge against the Martin regime for killing her mother. Sophie understood Carrie's motivations, but the thought of losing her young friend terrified Sophie.

"Watch over Rose while I'm gone," said Sophie.

"Where are you going?"

"I don't see any other way," Sophie said. "We need help. I'm going to national headquarters. It's time we took down Britwell and then Martin. We've been patient long enough."

"Then you'll need me on the inside."

"No, watch over Rose. Promise me you'll do that."

"I'll do both."

Sophie clenched her teeth and headed for the door. "I can't stop you, clearly. Be careful. And keep Chul updated. No one else, okay?"

Carrie smiled, her lips spreading apart, but the smile not reaching her eyes. Sophie felt bad for Junior and Britwell. They had no idea what force headed their way. This young woman was unstoppable. Carrie opened the door and poked her head out, checking the hallway. "Clear. Head up to the roof."

"I wasn't born yesterday, and didn't I teach you everything you know?"

"That you did," said Carrie, her hand on Sophie's shoulder as she pushed her out the door. "Take care of yourself. We need you alive."

Sophie nodded, then took off at a sprint. She'd have to chill for a few hours up on the cold, windy roof until patrols gave up their search for whoever had tripped the emergency exit alarm. They'd comb the building, awakening residents and searching apartments. Sophie felt bad for robbing everyone's sleep. But if she hadn't, they wouldn't live long anyway, their lives disrupted by Britwell's schemes.

Hours later, Sophie dragged herself into HQ, wanting nothing but a soft bed and pillow.

"Where have you been? I've been frantic. Patrols know someone was inside Little Asia and they think it was you." Alejandro's face was a thundercloud, the line between his eyebrows deep as a chasm.

"Yes, it was me," she pushed past him and headed for the conference room. "But I have the evidence we need to arrest Britwell for conspiracy once we find where he's storing everything. But that's easy enough. An operative or two can tail him to the hideout, probably outside Ivory."

"What are you talking about? Arrest Britwell? Are you out of your mind?" Alejandro loomed over her, outpacing Sophie into the conference room and blocking her entrance. She pushed past him anyway. "If we do that, we bring Junior and Supreme Commander Martin right down on our heads. You can't be serious."

Sophie sat in a swivel chair and swung herself back and forth. "Sit." She hated how he sometimes used his size to get his point across.

"I needed to see if Carrie had noticed anything at Central."

Sophie filled Alejandro in on the missing goods and the nighttime delivery from Junior's yacht, which Britwell had overseen.

"It has to all be true. He has guns, ammo, patrols uniforms, food, and who knows what else. Cigarettes to bribe the gate guards to let recruits out of the city. Don't you see? This is happening. He's trying to take over. Which means all our leaders are at risk."

"How would he know about our leadership? No way. Britwell might be on a power trip, but that doesn't mean he'll kill his opposition."

"Are you that blind or just purposely clinging to your safe, routine life? The evidence is right in front of you. Open your eyes, Alejandro."

Alejandro sunk into a chair at her side and took her hand. "I'm sorry I just don't see what you're seeing. Maybe we need to get someone on the inside. And if he's amassing a militia, who's to say it's not to help depose Martin instead? Maybe this Junior and the Secretary of State are in on it? Don't think Martin won't get wind of it. I don't want to be anywhere nearby when he finds out. It'll be a bloodbath. Don't you remember when the old Defense Secretary tried to assassinate him? Or when Canada and the IRT tried? It didn't end well for any of them."

If he weren't one of their underground leaders, Sophie would argue more. She squeezed his hand and let go. She'd have to do this on her own. Show him what he couldn't see, even though it stared him in the face.

"Give me a few weeks," she said. "In the meantime, keep an eye on Rose."

"What are you doing, Sophie?"

"What no one else can or will do. Getting help."

She stood, cutting off his arguments and questions, and headed to the women's dorm, sleep on her mind, though she doubted her swirling thoughts would leave her alone tonight. If she didn't act, Sophie feared the bloodbath from Britwell and Junior would set their cause back for generations. And that was unacceptable.

4

The wind in Sophie's hair had never felt so freeing before.

The motorcycle roared down the deserted back road in the equally deserted back country of the Appalachian foothills. She and Rich, one of the Queenstown Underground leaders who now lived full time at HQ and was often their city's representative to the national headquarters, had left Queenstown two days ago. She'd asked him to go with her to national HQ, to bring her concerns about Britwell and his schemes to their national leadership.

To her surprise, Rich and their other Queenstown Underground leaders had dissented from Alejandro and agreed to send them. Of course, Alejandro was furious at her, but he'd be fine once he realized she'd kept them all from dying in whatever power grab Britwell had in mind.

Rich leaned into a turn and Sophie scrambled to lean with him on one of the few still intact sections of pavement.

"A little warning next time?" she screamed over the wind.

Rich tilted his head to the side. "You should be watching the road, too," he answered with a yell. "There are more potholes than actual road around here."

She swatted him on the shoulder, then gripped his jacket.

Though Rich was an Ivory, he could've been her little brother for how they fought and nitpicked at each other.

Decades.

She'd known him and his now deceased wife for that long. She'd grieved the death of his wife and son with him. Rich's family had been yet another casualty from Hudson Britwell's power-grabbing schemes. He'd caused so much heartbreak over the years. Yet another reason Britwell needed to be taken down yesterday. If only they'd had enough evidence.

This could be their opportunity.

And Alejandro had just stood there, opposing her taking action.

She growled, and the wind swallowed the sound.

This area was gorgeous, the leafless trees standing like sentries over the hillsides. Deer, squirrels, and other small animals watched them pass, unafraid of humans or the loud machine they drove. Eagles, hawks, and turkey vultures flew and swooped over the trees, scanning for their next meal. She'd had to learn what those all were on her first and only trip to the national headquarters, since birds of prey avoided the city. Now that knowledge seemed like a treasure to Sophie.

Rich slowed the motorcycle to a crawl and swung onto a barely there footpath into the woods. He turned the bike off and steadied it while Sophie dismounted.

They'd have to walk from here, taking turns pushing the bike.

Spring would come soon to this area south of the FRA's recognized southern border at Queenstown. Supposedly, this region was in the dead lands, where nuclear bombs had eradicated life and made agriculture untenable. What the FRA's citizens didn't know was that this area had escaped any direct damage from the nuclear bombs dropped on the other side of the mountain range. It was the perfect place to hide a rebel movement. When Martin took over Queenstown at the end of the Great Civil War, this became the Underground's operational base.

Sophie hobbled after Rich, her legs still sore and vibrating from their four-hour motorcycle ride from the nearest Underground safe house. National HQ kept a series of safe houses stocked and secured — abandoned farm houses or condos in the many ghost towns in between the FRA's inhabited cities. She and Rich had feasted on rations bars and homemade canned goods heated over an ancient pre-Great Civil War propane camp stove, then slept on bare mattresses on the floor. It was a complicated system, but at least they had a means of escape, if it came to that. Though Sophie hated the idea of just leaving the FRA, abandoning its citizens to the whims of their madman dictator. She'd stay and fight to her death, even if she had to do it from the underground tunnels beneath Queenstown.

"Your turn," Rich said, offering her the handlebars.

"Thanks for saving the mud pit for me," she said, eyeing the stretch of dirt path ahead with its muddy peaks and troughs.

Someone had recently pushed another motorbike through this same section of mud, leaving long, deep tracks in the center of the path. She navigated the vehicle closer to the woods with its carpet of fallen leaves, crunching her way past the mud pit and back onto solid ground. They heaved the bike up a steep hill together, Rich whistling the safe messenger code, a two note tone mimicking the nightingale, to the sentries posted in the trees.

One whistled back with a wave.

They had arrived.

Rich took over pushing the cycle to the vehicle barn, while Sophie ventured toward the freshwater spring to clean off her hands.

"Hi!" her old friend, Candy, greeted her, a woven basket perched on her hip as she walked away from the stream. Sophie and Candy had met during Underground radio communications training and had only met on a video call once. The risk was far too great for frequent video calls.

"Good afternoon," said Sophie, greeting Candy with a slight dip of her chin. "Is it laundry day?"

Candy had been born in the Underground's secluded camp, and had learned to live off the land from an early age. Her father, Ian, was an Underground original. He'd fled Martin's rule on the same day Moses and Juli were caught, leading a group of survivors into the hills of the western Appalachian mountains. More than four decades later, the community was still going strong. Candy would never have been born in Queenstown, seeing as her father was Ivory and her mother was a Havana. Good thing the divisions that existed within the city didn't exist way out here.

Candy laughed. "Sure is. This is the last of it. My father is hanging a load of sheets over by the barns if you're looking for him. I'm sorry, I didn't know we were expecting guests."

"Last minute decision and Ruth wasn't available to send a message," said Sophie. "Though I guess I could've sent it. I didn't even think about it. We just left."

"We? Is Alejandro here, too? How did he get away?"

"No, I came with Rich."

Sophie fell into stride with Candy, heading toward the clearing by the barn where the community strung up their laundry to air dry. No washers or dryers existed here. No running water or electricity, either. They lived off the land and solar power, self-sustained with the supplement of supplies from the Underground's international allies.

As they walked through the compound, Candy greeted some community members, but shied away from others. Sophie's nose twitched.

"What's going on? I've never known you to not greet someone, but you've passed four people without even making eye contact," said Sophie. "You're the friendliest person I know, and frankly you annoyed me when we first met. This isn't like you."

Candy glanced around and subtly shook her head. "Not here."

Sophie crinkled her brows together and leaned in to take the basket from Candy. "Let me help you." As they passed the basket, Sophie whispered, "meet me tonight after dinner at the spring."

Candy nodded and strode ahead of Sophie, passing several people with only a brief wave.

As they hung the sheets on the line together, Sophie glanced around, noting who talked with whom and of the small groups gathered, but not intermingling. Some whispered in low tones, while others turned away, as if ignoring someone. A few looked ready to chew rocks, while others glanced furtively around, as if they were being hunted.

This wasn't the Underground Sophie knew and loved. Divided, suspicion rampant. She resolved to get to the bottom of this before it destroyed their shot at freedom.

5

S ophie enjoyed the silent cave corridors that evening, a thick wool blanket wrapped tightly around her shoulders as she strolled the halls. Rich had also noticed the murmuring and had vowed to corner his now deceased father's best friend, Manuel, and find out the truth, while Sophie worked on Candy. Perhaps with information from two perspectives, they could piece together what was wrong with the Underground's headquarters community.

Four and a half decades ago, Ian had led a small group out of the city that would become Queenstown. They had met up with Manuel and another group of stragglers to come here. Almost fifty refugees had settled in a secluded, forgotten saltpeter cave system hidden deep in the Appalachian hills. Prized during the first civil war for the raw materials of gunpowder, the world of the twenty-first century had moved on from the poverty-striken and flood-prone area of the Appalachian foothills. It had been the perfect place to hide a rebellion.

The rebels had learned to live off the land and the sun. Their water came from the nearby stream and they grew crops and raised livestock in adjacent fields.

Eventually, Ian and Manuel had established contact with other refugees who'd fled to the Independent Republic of Texas and the massive refugee camps inside Canada, now called the Protected Region of Minnesota.

Their allies had smuggled in guns, vehicles, protective body armor, and other items necessary to stage a rebellion. They'd also sent solar-powered batteries, providing the only source of electricity for the camp.

But forty-five years later, the Federated Republic of America and Martin remained untouched. Still kept their people divided into ethnic areas, locked behind impregnable walls away from each other, away from working together for their freedom.

But the Underground had a plan.

And this undercurrent of division would ruin it if Sophie and Rich didn't defuse the bomb before it blew up in their face and took them all down.

Sophie emerged from the cool, dark cave into the even cooler twilight air and breathed in the earthy scent of the forest which wrapped around the cave's entrance. She nodded to the sentry on duty.

"Don't go too far," the young woman said, a shotgun slung across her chest and her hands tucked in her woven pants pockets. "Curfew is in twenty-five minutes. Everyone must be inside by then."

"Thank you," said Sophie. "I understand."

She hurried down the rock face and along a well-worn dirt path. When she reached the stream, Candy sat along its banks, her bare toes curling into the soil. Sophie didn't understand how her friend could stand walking around barefoot in this chill.

"Hey," she said, sitting next to Candy on the hardened ground.

A warm hand covered her mouth, and Sophie lunged forward to bite down on it and throw her would be captor over her shoulder and into the stream.

"Hush," Candy said in a low tone. "It's Hugh, the British ambassador to the Underground. But he can't be seen meeting with you."

Sophie's shoulders sank down, and she relaxed her hold on his arm. Sophie held a thumbs up, and Hugh released her.

She turned toward Candy and saw Hugh's hulking form wreathed in the shadows of the nearby trees. "So, tell me what's going on and why Hugh needs to talk with me like this," she said, her eyes fixed on Candy.

"It's bad," said Candy. "Ian and Manuel are stuck in the middle between Sera and Charles. Sera thinks the regime knows about this place, while Charles is locked in la-la land, completely ignoring the signs that we've been outed and insisting we stay here."

"That's not all," said Hugh, leaning forward into the dim twilight, his huge form pressing against Sophie's shoulder. "I think Sera is right, but how she knows what she knows is very fishy. Britain has no intel, the IRT is tight-lipped, and your people in Minnesota haven't heard anything, either. So why does she think you've been compromised? Who's her information source and why won't she reveal them?"

He lifted his giant shoulders in a shrug as he spoke. Of Obsidian descent, Hugh clearly also had some Ivory blood in him, the evidence in his lighter skin tone and a jaw line which reminded her of an old friend and fellow Underground operative, Andrew Stewart.

But things were different in Britain. People mixed as they pleased, free to love and marry whomever they wished.

"Did she get a message from one of our operatives inside Martinsburg?" Sophie asked.

"The radio operator claims no," said Candy.

"Which means Sera's either completely paranoid or she has inside information."

Sophie swiveled her body away from Hugh, but spoke over her shoulder in his direction. "But you said you thought she was right. Why?"

"Too many strange coincidences," said Hugh. "For the first time ever, a prisoner escaped from the Martinsburg labor camp — and yes, we know these should've been disbanded decades ago but evidently they never were and we couldn't get observers in to verify that. But that's not the big problem. Somehow he found the camp here."

Sophie sucked in a breath, her hand flying to her mouth. "How?"

"Exactly," said Candy. "How is a great question. Our Martinsburg operatives don't know him. We have him in lockup."

"Too many coincidences. Wait until you hear why Rich and I came," Sophie said.

She explained about Britwell's schemes and his desire for power in Queenstown, how he'd assembled a militia with the approval of two Martin cabinet members.

Hugh spit out a word Sophie had never heard before. Must be a curse word in his home nation.

"They're working together?" Hugh asked.

"Who? Britwell and Junior MacBain? Yes," Sophie said. "From everything I could see it looks like Secretary of State Gonzalez is in on it, too."

Another unfamiliar word flew out of Hugh's mouth, making Sophie flinch.

"I have to go," said Hugh, vaulting to his feet and into the darkness of the surrounding forest. Away from the saltpeter cave and the warmth of a bed. Where was he headed?

"It's time to get inside," said Candy, her eye on the horizon as the sun's light faded behind the tall hill to the west.

Sophie stood, drawing Candy to her feet. "What does this mean?"

"I don't know, but I was so glad when I saw you," said Candy. "I have confidence you'll figure this out."

Sophie shook her head. Her friend might have confidence in Sophie, but how would Sophie find anything out when the others had all failed?

6

Sophie set her tray across from Rich and scanned her surroundings. Good, no one was close enough to overhear their conversation. She'd been trying to get him alone all day, but either Sera, Charles, or a community member had clung to Sophie non-stop, arguing their viewpoints and sharing rumors and gossip. She was emotionally wrung-out, nothing left to give. No level of reassurances or questioning had blunted the people's fear.

"This place," she said.

"I know," Rich replied. "It's changed a lot since I was here last. I don't even recognize it with all the factions, rumors, and accusations."

Sophie ate her vegetable stew, dipping the fluffy roll into the broth, while she told Rich about her conversation with both Candy and Hugh the night before.

"Wow, that jives with what Mani and Ian told me," Rich replied, his own dinner bowl licked clean. "Did you know Sera and Charles have been lovers for years? So it doesn't make sense for them to take opposing sides. Mani and Ian wonder if heading to the IRT could be a trap," he rested his chin in his palm and drew his eyebrows together.

"But there's more," he continued. "Mani was taking the prisoner, Joe, his meal the other day and walked in on Charles and Joe talking. They're holding Joe in a shed out past the barns, shielded from view.

So Mani overheard part of their conversation before he stepped out of the woods to confront Charles."

"Let me guess, they're collaborating?"

"Bingo," he said, Sophie frowning at the still unfamiliar-to-her Ivory game. Rich had promised to teach her someday, but Sophie was still waiting for the lesson. "Mani heard them refer to a common friend or acquaintance, no one here. Then they discussed scenarios for when the community leaves this camp."

"If Martin knows this place exists, why not just bomb it? He can send his Air Force hover planes here and it'd be gone in minutes."

Rich shrugged. "That's what I thought, too. And when I said that to Mani, he pointed out that Hugh is here."

Sophie nodded. Murdering one of their citizens would drag Britain into the fight. And the FRA wouldn't survive the world's biggest nuclear power's wrath. Not even the Chinese or Russians would dare to attack Britain.

"They can't annihilate the camp, so they're trying to draw the community into an ambush?" Sophie asked. "But why? After all these years and when the Martin regime probably knew the Underground existed? Why wait until now?"

"There you two are!" Sera claimed an empty seat at their table, smiling at them both.

Sophie's mouth dropped open, but she quickly shut it and smiled at Sera. "To what do we owe the pleasure of your company, Sera? We were just finishing dinner."

"I see. And I hope you've enjoyed the stew tonight?" Sera asked.

Sophie and Rich assured her the food was tasty, then exchanged wary glances. Everything in Sophie wanted to flee Sera's presence. She didn't trust the woman as far as she could throw her, and that wouldn't be far. Sera was a tall, muscular woman, far larger than Sophie's petite frame.

"I'm glad I found you two," Sera said. "Maybe you'll listen where Manuel and Ian are stubbornly refusing. We have to leave."

"I've heard you've advocated that," Rich said. "But why? Why is staying here dangerous?" Sera must not have cornered Rich today, unlike Sophie, who'd endured an hour of the woman's arguments and whining.

"That guy from Martinsburg has to be a regime plant!" Sera shrieked. "Which means Martin knows we are here!" Sera's exclamation drew the attention of the few people still inside the cafeteria, which was, without a doubt, her plan. She waved her hands wildly, painting a picture of Martin's bombs falling from the sky, penetrating even the solid rock walls of the saltpeter cave, and crushing the community and all its babies under tons of rock.

"Sera, let's reason this out," said Rich, his hands extended out to the woman. "You don't know for sure that this location is compromised. I heard Joe knew an older man inside the labor camp who pointed him in this direction. And it's someone Ian knew in the Great Civil War days. So perhaps he is a legitimate escaped prisoner."

Sera stood, flipping her metal chair to the ground, the sound echoing throughout the cavernous cafeteria space. "And how can we verify that? We can't! We have to flee or we'll die. No one listens. It's like they look at me, a black woman, and just disregard everything I say. It's just like what my Mom said happened in the old nation."

Sophie frowned. "This has nothing to do with you being black. Why would you think that? Sera, you're a leader in this community. Without your farming expertise, these people would starve. Can't you see that people are hesitant to leave the comfort of fields that produce, a clean water source, and the warmth of the underground cavern?"

"You, too? I can't believe this. And here I thought we women could stick together against the men," said Sera, right before she stomped off.

Sophie turned to Rich. "Something wasn't right about that."

"She got way too upset, way too quickly," said Rich. "Usually she's cool, calm, and collected. Nothing ruffles her."

"She's up to something, for sure," said Sophie. "Everything points to it."

"We need to trail her," said Rich as he stood up and pushed back his chair. "Guard my six."

Rich handed his Beretta revolver to Sophie, and she tucked it into her jacket pocket. Its weight smothered a little of her anxiety.

"What are you doing?" Sophie raised her brows at his favorite weapon, extending it back toward him.

"I'm going to follow her," said Rich over his shoulder. "And confront her on the lies. Keep that."

Sophie counted to one-hundred then followed him. As she passed the guard at the cave entrance, he reminded her curfew would start shortly. Here she was, leaving the warm comfort of the cave right before curfew for the second night in a row. Sophie huffed out a breath and wrapped her jacket more tightly around her. The late winter air in the mountains was definitely cooler than she'd expected. Sophie kept Rich in view as they wove along a well-worn path in the woods toward the barns. She knew where they headed — the shed where Joe remained imprisoned.

Interesting.

Sophie ducked off the path and into woods, hiding behind a concealing thicket as Rich emerged into the small clearing. The wan rising moonlight combined with the remnants of the sun's last gasp were barely bright enough for Sophie to identify Sera and Rich, when a taller, thin man joined them from inside the shed.

Sophie bit back a curse and drew her weapon, quickly flicking off the safety. She knelt, her knees sinking into the dead, wet leaves covering the ground. She crawled forward until her elbows rested against a fallen tree. Sophie aimed her revolver at Charles, but he shifted, putting Rich into the line of fire.

"Come on, move," she whispered.

Voices filtered to her through the woods. Shouts of anger and accusation, Rich pointing his finger first at Sera, then at Charles.

A hulking man emerged from inside the shed and a glint of metal was Sophie's only warning. A blast echoed through the trees — not even a silencer completely silences a gunshot — and Sophie rocketed to her feet and over the fallen tree, her revolver up and aimed at Joe. Rich tumbled to the ground.

Sophie halted as Joe swung his weapon toward her.

"What did you see? Is someone out there?" Sera asked, spinning to face the woods, her gaze searching the darkness.

Both Sera and Charles had drawn weapons, and were fanning out away from Rich's unmoving body. Sophie covered the barrel of her revolver with her free hand, then froze.

"I must've imagined it," said Joe. "No one's there." He turned back to Rich and hoisted her friend's limp body over his shoulder.

"Is he dead?" Charles asked.

At Joe's nod, Charles said, "Good riddance. I hated him. Too nosy. Always pressing for details and challenging my ideas."

"Darling, sometimes your ideas need to be challenged," said Sera, grabbing Charles' hand as the trio disappeared behind the shed.

Sophie stared after them in shock.

Sera and Charles definitely together. Joe most assuredly not an escaped labor camp prisoner, but rather, an armed assassin. Their voices faded into the night and Sophie collapsed to the ground, tears rolling down her face.

Rich, someone who'd been like a brother to her for decades, was gone.

Dead.

And she hadn't fired a single shot. From his gun, which he'd given to her. She was supposed to have covered him. But she'd failed to see the threat until it was too late.

Not that Sophie would've survived against three armed assailants.

Her tears rolled down her cheeks and soaked the shirt under her jacket, chilling Sophie and making her long for the warmth of the cave. But she didn't dare move. She needed to know where they'd tossed her friend.

Rich deserved a proper burial and justice.

***

After the trio had been gone for a few torturous minutes, Sophie emerged from the darkness and protection of the woods and walked around the shed's perimeter. A trail in the woods sloped uphill, away from the cave and the stream. She threaded through the woods about ten yards in until she heard footsteps shuffling in the night.

Sophie curled herself into a ball on the ground, disappearing into the darkness like a wraith.

Sera and Charles passed her first, whispering to each other low enough that Sophie couldn't make out their conversation.

She waited and waited, counting to nearly one-thousand before Joe passed, his footfalls nearly silent on the dirt trail. She allowed another fifteen minutes to pass, counting slowly to herself the entire time and resisting the urge to run down the path.

Sophie had decided the way must finally be clear when soft footfalls sounded through the night. Joe returned, creeping down the pathway and scanning both sides of the woods.

He had definitely seen her before and now he was hunting.

For her.

The bulky man held a long rifle in the low, ready position, his finger near the trigger, and she knew without a doubt if he discovered her, she'd be dead.

Sophie held her breath and froze as he passed not once, not twice, but three times. Finally, he headed back toward the shed.

Sophie waited a full hour before moving one slow, excruciating step at a time through the woods.

It took her hours, but by dawn she stood amid a dense fog at the edge of a deep ravine. Sophie knelt and, through the wisps of fog, stared at the ravine's bottom.

Rich's body lay draped over a pile of rocks, his neck at an unnatural angle.

She cursed, slamming her fist into the ground.

There's no way he'd survived being dumped over the side of a cliff after a shot to the head.

Rich was gone.

And Sophie would be next unless she proceeded with extreme caution.

She trekked back through the woods, the bright sunlight of dawn casting long shadows among the trees. Her mind played tricks on her.

A wet leaf became a glint of metal. A thick bush turned into Joe lying in wait.

When she'd finally reached the first barn, Sophie nearly fainted in relief. Hugh groomed a horse, a frown enhancing his tough exterior. She caught his gaze from behind an elm and motioned for him to join her.

Hugh looked around, then threw the horse's reins around the post, and strolled into the woods.

"Where have you been?" he asked. "You and Rich both missed curfew last night. Everyone was talking about it at breakfast, saying you'd just up and left."

"Rich is dead," said Sophie, crossing her arms over her chest. She'd never be warm again. "Charles set Joe free, and Joe murdered Rich. Sera watched the whole thing, then celebrated his death. They're conspiring together. Leaving is definitely a trap, but staying might be, too."

That same curse from before flew from Hugh's mouth again.

Sophie shook and her teeth clacked together.

"You've been out all night," he said, draping an arm around her. "We need to get you warm. And then let's find Manuel and Ian."

"Forget about what I need. We need to arrest Sera and Charles and take Joe into custody again," said Sophie. "Then we need to get out of here like a bat from the cave at dusk."

"But the community has to decide all that," Hugh said. "Let's find Ian and Manuel. They'll know what to do."

Sophie groaned. Yes, she knew the community had to make any major decision. That's why there was so much division. No one agreed. Everyone had their own ideas. They were at a stalemate. Maybe Rich's death would change that.

"Will you be ok on your own?" Hugh asked. "It's better if we split up to find them. Ian will be out with a hunting party, and Manuel would be with the livestock."

"Of course, I'm fine," she said. "I'm a grown woman. But I'm not traipsing through the woods any longer. I'll head inside and grab some food, then find Manuel."

"I'll find Ian," Hugh gave her a thumbs up and looked at her with pity, as if he might comfort her in her grief.

Sophie stepped back, putting distance between them. She couldn't stand even a hint of his sympathy.

"Let's go get justice for Rich," she said, not bothering to wave goodbye as she circled the barn and headed toward the saltpeter cave entrance.

7

"**I**'m in shock," said Manuel, a hand stroking his mostly-gray beard. "I didn't think Charles or Sera were capable of violence like this." He wiped his palm down his cheek and rested his hand on the wooden conference room table.

The door was closed as Sophie shared with Manuel, Ian, and Hugh every gory detail from the night before. She couldn't believe it either. They'd all worked together for decades. This betrayal struck deep in her soul and a part of her blamed Joe for turning the two Underground national leaders away from their movement's values and objectives.

As if counter-point to that thought, Charles's words saying he'd always hated Rich came to mind. How long had he been a regime sympathizer? Sophie marveled at how Charles had avoided detection for years, rising into leadership, a powerful and well-respected voice within the community and beyond.

"We need an assembly," Ian said. "Tonight." He stood, pushing his metal chair back from the table in one fluid movement. "My gut is that we'll leave pretty quickly after we find those three. Maybe they'll make it easier on us and show up for the assembly."

Hugh shook his head. "They're in the wind. I tracked them at least four miles away, then had to turn back to find your hunting party."

"Let's all meet right before the assembly to plan how this will go," Manuel said. He leaned his chair onto his back legs, his hands gripping his long curls. "I miss him already."

"Me too," said Sophie, a pit yawning open in her chest. She shoved it aside. They had no time for grief now.

Manuel's chair came crashing back onto all four legs and he pressed on his thighs to stand. "Be careful, Sophie. We don't know if there are other traitors in our midst, people working alongside Sera and Charles. Don't hint you know what happened to Rich or you'll have a giant target on your back."

She knew a lot of things, most of it a secret. Sophie was a master of secrets, guarding them like a treasure of gold and silver coin.

Then there were the things she needed to expose, but only in due time. And it wasn't yet time. If the Underground couldn't handle a simple labor camp escapee, how would they ever handle the explosive news Sophie held inside?

"I'm starving and I need to clean up," she said.

"Um," Ian said, his gray hair shining in the dim candlelight while his face remained in shadows. "You know it's not bathing day, right?"

Sophie waved a hand and stood. Of course she knew it wasn't bathing day, the one afternoon when the camp broke into male and female ranks and the nearby lake became an enormous bathtub. A simple washcloth and a bucket of soapy water in the women's bathroom would meet her needs.

"Maybe you shouldn't go anywhere alone," said Hugh. "This Joe guy sounds like a skilled military operator. And I doubt the camp's meager security would even slow him down."

"I'll be fine," said Sophie. "I'm armed and I'm not going far. I promise to keep my wits about me."

She left the conference room, heading first for a meal. When Sophie entered the cafeteria, the main room was deserted, but voices filtered to her from the kitchen area. She stepped into the hot kitchen and her mouth immediately watered at the earthy scent of sauteed mushrooms and steaming rice wafting out of the various pots.

"Well, look who the barn cat dragged in!" the head cook said, raising an eyebrow at Sophie, her gaze drifting over Sophie's hair and clothing. Sophie's hair was in a tangle from pulling at it throughout the night. Her face was puffy, and mud and leaf stains dotted her clothing. She had never cared less about her appearance in her life.

"I missed breakfast," said Sophie. "Any chance you all have something left?"

"Lunch is almost ready," the cook said. "I'll make you a plate. Grab yourself some coffee from the carafe over there. It's probably still warm. Was getting ready to toss it, but no sense in that when someone really needs it."

The woman laughed, her skinny shoulders shaking as she stirred the mushrooms in the pan. A large vat of already-cooked mushrooms sat to the side, steam filtering up to mix with the smoke from the wood fire before disappearing up one of the many smoke holes in the saltpeter cave.

"Got it," said Sophie.

She grabbed a thick white mug and poured the last of the carafe's contents into her cup, doctoring the dark brew with a large spoonful of sugar and a healthy pour of cream. Sophie hated coffee, but couldn't deny she needed the warmth and the caffeine. What she wouldn't do for a cup of hot green tea right now.

She sat at the nearest table and sipped at the brew, grimacing at its bitterness. Wondering what was taking the kitchen crew so long to bring her a plate, Sophie stood and everything spun.

Strong arms banded around her shoulders, steadying her.

"I've got you," a familiar voice said.

Sophie struggled to place why that voice was familiar, to grasp the threads of why her brain screamed to run. She turned to see who held her and the world went black.

8

S ophie stirred in her sleep, wondering why her body ached practically everywhere. Had she lifted the laundry basket wrong? No, that wasn't right. The laundry was days ago.

Then she remembered and squeezed her eyelids shut.

Joe had murdered Rich.

Sophie had watched them drag Rich's body off and found it tossed over the edge of a ravine.

Then she'd spent the night outside.

But she wasn't lying on a thin mattress in the women's dormitory. Keeping her eyes shut, Sophie cataloged her body and her surroundings.

Aching shoulders. A hip pressed into a hard surface. Dry mouth and a churning stomach. Cold stone under her cheek. Her hands bound tightly behind her. That explained her aching shoulders.

Dry mouth, nausea. What had she eaten last? She remembered the smell of sauteed mushrooms, but not the taste.

The cook had told her to drink something while waiting. Then Sophie remembered the bitter taste of the coffee and nausea overtook her again.

If Sophie survived this, she'd never drink coffee again. Ever.

The pieces slammed together, and Sophie knew what had happened. She'd been drugged, kidnapped, and left bound.

So where were her captors? And where was she?

Faint voices filtered to Sophie. "I told you to kill her," a female voice — was that Sera?

"Where's the fun in that?" a man replied.

Sophie hadn't heard Joe clearly the other night, but the voice's depth and timbre matched the man's physique. Whatever Joe thought of as fun caused Sophie's heart to fly into high gear.

Sophie cracked her eyelids and squinted against the sunlight streaming into the cave. Three dark figures stood at the entrance.

Sera gestured with her hands, but faced away from Sophie.

Did whatever they gave her also affect her hearing? Sophie felt like she was underwater.

Sera and the second male — presumably Charles — walked out of the cave.

A muscled man, Joe, turned to face Sophie. "I see you're awake," he said. "You'll be the perfect bait. But I need a few things for our journey. Don't go anywhere." He chuckled and shook his head. "As if you can."

As soon as the man disappeared down the rock face, Sophie scrambled to her knees. Thick chains bolted into the cave's wall secured her ankles and limited her movement. But the good thing about caves were the rock shards scattered everywhere. She scooted around to grasp one with her right hand and started in on the plastic zip ties binding her wrists. Thoughts of how she'd figure out where she was and find her way back to camp filled her mind.

Sophie grunted as her grip slipped, and the stone cut into her left wrist. She blinked tears back and told herself to stay focused.

Feeling around, she picked the rock up again and sawed until the zip ties burst apart. She rubbed her bleeding wrist, wiping the thin stream of blood on her shirt. She'd be fine for now.

Sophie patted herself down, searching for anything slim to pick the thick lock on the chains.

Nothing, not even a zipper pull.

She dropped her head into her hands, a solitary tear staining her shirt.

Forget about finding her way back to camp. She had to free herself before that beast came back or she was good as dead.

***

Sophie had almost given up hope of freeing her ankles from the metal shackles secured to the thick chain embedded into the cave's stone wall when a scuffle outside made her go still. She dropped to the ground, her hands behind her back as if she hadn't already escaped the zip ties.

A gunshot startled her, and dread crawled up her throat. She was going to die. And maybe not so quickly.

"Sophie!" a familiar voice called out, and she almost wept with relief.

"Over here, Hugh," she croaked out. She cleared her throat. "Sorry," she said, in the same level of croak. "Water?"

"Let's get you out of here first," he said. "Thankfully the bloke had the keys on him."

Sophie sat up and Hugh unlocked the thick shackles from around her ankles. She rubbed the skin under them, thankful to see she hadn't broken the skin in struggling to free herself.

"Are these yours?" Hugh handed Sophie her boots, and she quickly put them on.

"Ok, let's go," he lifted her to her feet and dragged her away from the cave. Blood pooled under and flowed away from Joe's still body, a thin river down the smooth rock face leading up to the cave.

Sophie spat on him as they passed. "Good riddance. That's for killing Rich, though you deserved a slow, torturous death."

Hugh patted Sophie's shoulder and turned her toward a dense thicket of thorny shrubs. "Charles and Sera left, but that gunshot might bring them back," he said. "Let's double back through the woods instead of using their path. This isn't the first time they've been back and forth."

He draped his jacket over the bush, ushering her past the thorns before pushing through and then reclaiming his jacket on the other side. He kept his hand on her arm the entire time.

"I need to pee," Sophie said.

"Go ahead," Hugh gestured to a nearby tree. "Stay close. That drug isn't totally out of your system and I don't want you taking a fall."

"I'm not peeing with you right here," Sophie said.

"I'll turn my back and sing quietly then. I won't hear a thing."

Sophie raised her eyebrow at the younger man, but eventually relented. He wouldn't leave her alone, and maybe he was right. She wobbled more than a little as she squatted, bracing herself on the thick tree trunk.

Hugh sang quietly, the words and tune unfamiliar. At least he sang on-key and his voice wasn't terrible.

When she was done, Sophie stood. "What song was that?"

"Oh, that's a British patriotic song," he said. "God Save The Queen."

Sophie grunted. "Can I have water now?"

"While we walk," he handed her a metal flask. "But don't guzzle. You'll just throw it up. I think they gave you Rohypnol. When you didn't show up before curfew, I searched your quarters, then Sera's and Charles's, who also didn't make it into the cave before curfew. I found a full bottle of it shoved under Sera's mattress."

"How did she get it?"

Hugh shrugged, and his shoulder brushed hers. He kept his hand on her elbow as if she were an old woman. And didn't it make her feel every year of her age that, without his steadying hand, she'd be on the forest floor?

If she didn't make it back alive, Alejandro would have her neck. Sometimes the man drove her crazy and other times she loved him with every fiber of her being. She had to get back to warn everyone of the horrible truth.

They traipsed through the dense trees and underbrush for a few hours, Hugh stopping every so often to check a thin metal compass before the barns came into view.

Sophie breathed a sigh and relaxed her shoulders.

"Not so soon," he said. "We could be walking into an ambush. I suspect Charles and Sera were coming back to either convince Mani and Ian of their way, or kill them."

Sophie hung her head. She was so tired. Tired of constantly fighting people to do what was right. Tired of fighting the regime. Tired of hiding and being told "not yet."

"So, what's the plan? If we can't waltz right in and take over, how's this going to work?"

"First off, you need this," Hugh held out a revolver to her and Sophie stepped away, her hands raised.

"Was that Joe's?"

Hugh nodded, his lips thinned and his eyes on her.

"I can't. Where's mine? Or the one Rich gave me? I had his with me last I remembered."

"This was all I found. You have to," he said, shoving the revolver into her hands. "It's only a tool. In your hands, you'll use it for good. There are three rounds loaded." He held out a handful more, and she took it with a frown.

"Ok, but only because they took mine and there's no other choice." Sophie loaded rounds into the empty slots and tucked the few spares into her inner jacket pocket. "Let's do this."

She chambered a round and gestured for Hugh to take the lead.

9

S ophie darted into the entrance to the saltpeter cave.

"Why isn't the guard here?" Hugh said as he pushed past her, his revolver drawn and in the low-ready position, tucking her in behind his broad back.

"There's a lot of shouting," Sophie said, trying to catch her breath and see past Hugh.

It had been years since she'd run that far. Sprints in the tunnels were one thing, but running for over an hour was quite another. Hugh bladed his body against the cool cave wall and peeked around the corner.

Sophie followed him, running straight toward the pandemonium.

Residents screamed at each other, dragging children up the hallway leading to their residences. Their fear coated Sophie's tongue like rancid oil.

Candy raced toward them.

"What in Martin's macrocosm is going on?" Sophie blanched at using Rose's favorite slang phrase and clamped a hand over her mouth.

"They killed him. Charles killed him," Candy's eyes darted around the cave and she hunched over, as if trying to duck. "The hunting party found Rich's body in a ravine, Sophie. He's dead. I'm so sorry. And then, when they told Charles, he shot the man who told him," her eyes grew even wider as she shared the story. "And bam, Daniel dropped to the floor dead."

A lone tear trailed down her cheeks. Sophie wrapped her friend into a tight hug, telling herself this physical contact was essential and to swallow her own discomfort.

"I know he's dead. I saw Joe murder him. Charles and Sera were there, dumped Rich's body, then kidnapped me, and left me for dead. But Hugh killed Joe, and I escaped. Where are your Dad and Manuel? We've got to find them fast. Before Sera and Charles kill them, too, and turn this place over to Martin."

Candy stiffened at that last sentence. "What about my children?"

"Listen first, where did you last see your leaders?"

"I... I don't know," Candy's gaze bounced frantically around the saltpeter cave entrance. She ripped out of Sophie's grasp and sprinted toward the women's dormitory and her teenaged daughter, no doubt.

Sophie breathed deeply. "We have to find them, Hugh, or this place — and everyone here — will die. Then we have to evacuate. Martin's hover planes could be already on their way."

"Agreed," he said. "This is chaos, which tells me Sera and Charles are probably holding Manuel and Ian somewhere. They might even be dead. If either of them were here, they'd take charge and calm everyone. But that's not happening."

"The flow of traffic is all toward the residential wing," said Sophie, turning to the opposite hallway. "Let's clear the classrooms and meeting rooms first."

She raised her revolver and led them down the candlelit classroom hallway. They worked together to clear the first few meeting rooms, small spaces meant for groups of four to six, with a blackboard and chairs.

Sophie's frustration mounted. Maybe they'd chosen the wrong hallway and should search the residences instead? The realization Sophie and Hugh were walking into a trap didn't dim Sophie's desire to find her leaders. Not at all. If anything, she wanted to spring that trap as soon as humanly possible.

Sophie stood on one side of the council room door, the last meeting room in this hallway, hoping against hope that this is where they'd find Manuel and Ian, hopefully alone, working out an evacuation plan. Hugh posted up on the other side, his hand on the knob. He mouthed a countdown before they simultaneously burst into the room, weapons sweeping the space.

Of course, Sophie couldn't be that lucky.

The two leaders sat at the conference table, their hands zip tied to the chair armrests. Presumably their feet were also zip tied, explaining why neither struggled to get free.

Sera, who had been closer to the door, dove under the table and scrambled away from Sophie.

Charles stood like a statue behind Manuel's chair, his revolver unwavering against Manuel's temple. Charles's expression was blank, as if he were tired of waiting for them to show up.

"Hello, Charles. Hello Sera. Your hideout bored me. Figured I'd join you here," Sophie said as she kicked aside a chair and locked Sera in her revolver's sights.

Hugh flanked the table to Sophie's left, his revolver steady on Charles.

"I see. Hugh, thank you for escorting our guest here today. You're dismissed. I'm sure you have better things to do," Sera said, her voice muffled. She crawled backward out from under the table and away from Sophie, to stand behind Ian, who winced at the revolver now digging into his back.

Sophie shifted to keep Sera locked in her sights and her body between both Charles and Sera and the door into the hallway.

"I'm not going anywhere," said Hugh with a wry chuckle, his revolver held steady.

"Drop your weapons and maybe you'll survive today." Charles's laugh was deep-throated, his smile not extending beyond the upturned corners of his lips.

"Oh, we'll survive."

Manuel raised his left eyebrow at Sophie and then darted his gaze toward his left. Sophie pinched her brows together, wondering what he was trying to communicate.

But when Manuel exploded to his left, understanding dawned and Sophie pulled the trigger, her bullet penetrating Sera's shoulder and throwing the woman backward onto the floor.

Then, everything happened all at once.

Ian also threw his weight to the side, toppling his chair and sheltering him underneath both the table and the heavy wooden chair.

Hugh's bullet, meant for Charles, embedded harmlessly in the wall behind where Charles had once stood. Charles pushed past Manuel, then darted out of the conference room.

Sera leaped over the conference table, blood spurting from her left shoulder as she fired one-handed at Sophie. But Sophie was already on her way to the floor and the bullet whizzed by her ear.

Sophie rolled under the table, then vaulted to her feet next to where Manuel lay on his side, his legs in the air where they were zip tied to the chair's legs.

"Go get them!" Ian yelled, as Hugh cut Ian's hands and ankles free.

"Not until you two are free," said Sophie.

Hugh tossed her his knife, and Sophie made quick work of the zip ties on Manuel's wrists and ankles. He rubbed his hands, then pushed to stand alongside Ian.

"They got the drop on us and confiscated our weapons," Ian said. "They've killed enough people. I need my spare."

"Me too," Manuel said. "You two start in the cafeteria. They'll likely be grabbing supplies from the pantry and storage areas before they leave, if they don't have allies already doing that. We'll meet you by the motorcycle barn."

The two men sprinted out of the conference room and down the hallway ahead of Hugh and Sophie, turning into the residential wing, which had fallen eerily silent.

"We got this," said Hugh, leading the way toward the large cafeteria. His voice echoed and bounced off the cave's stone walls.

Where had everyone gone? And who were Sera's and Charles's accomplices? Not knowing whom they could trust made Sophie's back itch with the threat of a bullet.

10

S ophie strode into the food services area, following an obvious blood drip trail.

It was almost lunchtime and workers should've been stirring large pots of stew over the cook fires in the center of the space. Instead, the kitchen stood empty, a pot boiling over. Sophie ran into the kitchen, grabbed protective mitts, lifted the heavy stew pot off the cook fire, and placed it on the stone ground.

Disaster averted, at least for now.

She headed to where Hugh darted from the shadows of a wall-mounted oil lantern inside the cafeteria and into the dark storage area, motioning for her to hurry.

Sophie entered the hallway, feeling her way along a wall. There were no wall-mounted candle lanterns or low-energy floor lighting scattered throughout the rest of the cave.

Hugh handed her a small flashlight. "It's too quiet back here," he whispered.

"More bodies?"

"That's what I'm concerned about. Where did the kitchen staff go?"

She hummed in agreement. "No clue. Lead on."

He clicked his flashlight on, covering the light with his left hand, his revolver in the low-ready position in his right. Sophie searched into the dry goods pantry, while Hugh remained in the hallway to cover her.

"Clear," she whispered.

They repeated the process from one storage area to the next, stepping over bags of dried food and other supplies littering the aisles in every room.

"They were definitely here. No telling what's missing," Hugh said as they cleared the last supply room where cooking utensils and spare pots lay scattered on the floor.

"They must've created a racket with all this."

"It's a wonder no one came to investigate." Sophie stepped over an empty ammo box and stray bullets as they headed toward the rear emergency exit from the saltpeter cave. It was much smaller, the hallway allowing single file passage only.

Sophie looked back at Hugh, who ducked his head to not ram it into the uneven ceiling and the reinforcing wooden planks. Near the exit the narrowing hallway forced them to turn sideways, a classic chokepoint that would be easy for the residents to defend in the event of an attack.

"They have to be heading to the motorcycles or transport barns," said Hugh. "I wonder if it's just the two of them or if they have followers."

"Knowing those two, they're saving their own hides," said Sophie. Only cowards killed a man to protect their messed-up betrayal.

"I have an idea, then," said Hugh. "Let's take a shortcut through the woods."

"Through the woods? Won't we get lost?"

Hugh chuckled. "Not me. I've traversed these woods off-trail day and night. It was the only way to get secure messages off to my bosses in Britain."

Sophie raised her eyebrows at the admission that he could navigate the woods at night. Hugh had to be more of a special operative than a politician. A military man skilled in warfare and spy craft. She shouldn't be surprised after how easily he'd dispatched the hulking Joe.

As they headed out of the bright sunlight and into the dense woods, Sophie knew where they were — near the laundry lines and the path leading to the horse corrals. They darted past those areas, the air a silent tomb when shouts and conversations would normally fill the space at this time of day.

"Step exactly where I step." Hugh set a quick pace through the underbrush, Sophie lengthening her steps to match his boot prints.

Hugh headed roughly north, the mossy sides of trees at their backs, away from the laundry area, the horse corrals, and the animal barns. They threaded through the trees and around thick snarls of bramble bushes for about ten more minutes before she saw the rear entrance of the motorcycle garage.

"Stay here and stay down," said Hugh. "I'm going to draw them out."

"That's a stupid idea. You're a better shot than me," said Sophie. She grabbed for his shirt but caught nothing but air.

Hugh had already stepped out of the dark, thick underbrush into the bright sunlight.

Charles exited the garage door, a rifle leveled at Hugh's chest. "Thought you could stop us? You've made a critical mistake coming alone, Hugh."

Sophie bladed her body behind a tree trunk, scanning the shadowed woods.

Where were Manuel and Ian? They should be here with an armed squad by now, right? How had they beaten them? She silently cursed that shortcut through the woods. Sophie peeked around the trunk to see Hugh slowly raise his hands.

"Even if you kill me, the others will stop you," said Hugh.

Sophie crept through the dark woods, rolling through her feet and watching for twigs. One crack and Charles would know Hugh had backup. Then it would be game over.

"Drop the gun. You aren't leaving. I won't let you ruin what's taken years to accomplish."

Hugh slowly complied.

When she'd finally worked her way around the clearing, Sophie emerged from the tree line behind Charles and ducked into the barn's shadow. She raised her revolver, taking aim at Charles's back.

"Stop right there, Charles. We have you surrounded," Sophie commanded.

Charles spun, his rifle discharging aimlessly as he searched the dark woods twenty feet to her right.

Sophie sprinted at Charles, knocking his rifle to the ground with a strong uppercut. She kicked him in the chest, throwing his weight into Hugh, who threw Charles to the ground and onto his stomach.

Hugh pinned the man's arms behind his back and secured them with a zip tie, the sound like music to Sophie's ears. Hugh nodded toward the barn, gesturing he'd cover her.

Sophie peeked around the entrance, scanning the darkness. Keeping her back firmly against the outside slats, Sophie shouted into the enormous structure. "Sera, it's time to surrender," Sophie said, her voice echoing off metal motorcycle replacement parts and the metal repair lifts.

"Never!"

Sophie led with her revolver into the barn, but quickly ducked back around when she saw a group working their way in the front entrance doors, one covering the rest as they advanced like skilled patrols penetrating a criminal's home.

"Sera," Ian said.

Sophie breathed a sigh of relief and nodded at Hugh where he sat on Charles's back.

"I have you in my sights. Drop your weapon."

A guttural scream behind her made Sophie spin. Hugh had Charles in a headlock, but Charles had somehow busted the zip ties and now struggled against Hugh's grasp, his lips turning an ominous shade of purple.

Sophie scanned the woods, holding up a raised hand at Manuel's approach around the side. Quiet descended across the clearing.

"He's not dead, just out," said Hugh, standing up and dusting off his jeans. "He fought like an alleycat."

"Not sure what that is, but I'll take your word for it," said Sophie, walking over to join Hugh. They didn't have cats in Little Asia. Not even as pets. Pets were a waste of resources according to their area's traditions.

Hugh dropped an arm around Sophie's shoulders and squeezed. "Are you okay? He didn't hit you, right?"

She shrugged out of his grasp and flicked her revolver's safety on. "I'm fine. The bullet missed wide."

Hugh secured Charles's wrists with zip ties once again, clenching them more tightly than before.

"What are we going to do with them?"

Sera's screams echoed out of the barn.

"Secured and clear," came the shout from inside.

"This is loco," Manuel said.

"What do we do now?"

Ian joined them. "We gather everyone and have a community meeting. We vote. But I don't think we can stay. That's clear as day now."

"But perhaps there's another option you all hadn't considered before," Sophie said, frowning at Hugh's fist extended toward her.

"What's that for?"

"Never mind," Hugh said. "I'll teach you later, old bird."

"I'm not old," Sophie said.

"Yes, you are, but that's okay," said Hugh. "You kept up today."

Manuel wiped his face with the back of his hand and ignored their banter. "Our people must be scared out of their minds. And I want to hear your idea, Sophie. While we walk."

"They were, yes," said Sophie. "But knowing you two are unharmed will calm them. That and a plan. Or at least I hope."

As they walked back, Sophie shared her idea in low tones. It was a tremendous gamble, but maybe this could be the break they needed to not only protect Queenstown but also finally win freedom for the Federated Republic of America.

11

S ophie sat at a bench in the cafeteria, a bowl of only slightly burned bean soup in front of her. Good thing she'd taken the large pot off the cook fire or they'd all be going hungry. Or eating charred beans.

Ian carried a long bone horn out of the storage area and stood at the cafeteria entrance. He blew into the horn, making Sophie slap her hands over her ears. The low note echoed through the caverns, bouncing back with even lower echoes.

Workers exited the kitchen, wiping hands on aprons or towels and taking seats along a nearby bench. Other residents straggled in, dragging crying or wide-eyed children. Some of the younger men flinched when they saw Sera and Charles bound and gagged, their chairs placed in front of the large communal fire area. Sophie's knee bounced up and down, and she pressed a hand on her thigh and stilled the motion. No sense betraying to everyone how nervous she was at how the community would respond to her idea. They had few options, fewer than when she'd arrived. Would everyone blame her and Rich for stirring up trouble? Sophie snorted at that thought. No way she'd receive that blame, which lay squarely at Sera and Charles's feet.

When the stream slowed to a trickle, Ian clapped for attention. "Thank you for coming so quickly," he said. "And thank you for remaining calm during our earlier emergency, and for obeying our procedures."

They'd been calm? Sophie schooled her features to neutral so she wouldn't roll her eyes like a teenager. These residents had been anything but calm, but maybe Ian meant his words to reassure them now.

"Sera and Charles have killed two men in our midst," Ian said. "The first was Rich. Our hunting party discovered his body in a ravine, and his colleague, Sophie, witnessed his murder. The second is Daniel. Charles shot him in cold blood as our hunting group told him about finding the body. Little did we know that Charles and Sera had ordered not only Rich's death, but also Sophie's. Charles and Sera have pled guilty to these crimes."

Ian paused as murmurs ran through the community. Arguments peaked and fell, voices cutting off or rising up.

One young man stood and raised his hand. "How do we know Sophie didn't kill Rich herself then pin the blame on our leaders? Sera is my cousin and I don't believe she's capable of murder."

Sera nodded at him and sat up straighter.

Sophie walked to the front of the room. "Do I look like someone who could drag the body of a man twice my size over a mile and a half? Joe carried Rich's body. I followed through the woods, sick with grief. Rich was like a brother to me."

A hand on her shoulder stilled her argument, and Sophie fought to blink back tears. She. Did. Not. Cry. Ever. Yet, she had in the last few days and this would make one time too many.

"Furthermore," said Hugh, joining Sophie at the front of the room. "Sera drugged Sophie and she and Charles took her to a cave over several hours' hike away. I tracked them and, when I arrived, heard their intentions to also kill her. I subdued Joe, who was definitely a trained operative not some labor camp fugitive, and led Sophie back to the camp. By the time we returned, another man was murdered, and Sera and Charles had Ian and Manuel held at gunpoint. They would've killed the rest of your leaders, and why?"

Hugh turned to Charles. Charles shook his head, refusing to elaborate.

"I think it's because Charles and Sera are collaborating with Supreme Commander Martin," said Hugh.

"We discovered they had planned an ambush on our people had we fled to the IRT, and if we'd stayed?" Ian shrugged. "They'll be bombing us here any day."

The community let out screams and shrieks until Manuel put two fingers between his lips and a piercing whistle brought the room to silence once again. Alejandro could do the same thing and had refused to teach Sophie. But what a useful skill that was. She'd have to ask him again.

"We aren't here to vote on fleeing to the IRT or staying," said Manuel. "Those are no longer feasible. We are here to first vote on what to do with Sera and Charles. There are two options, given the rules of our community. First, execution. An eye-for-an-eye. They are complicit in the murders of two innocent men. You've heard the evidence already. Second, abandonment. We leave them here, bound and chained, and let the regime's bombs kill them."

Sera's eyes grew wide, and she strained against her bonds.

"There's no escape," said Ian. "You'll die either way. With one option you might have a chance."

The community debated openly, men and women standing to speak out for or against either option.

"We don't kill," one woman said.

"But they shouldn't be allowed to live after killing my Daniel," a woman with two young children clinging to her said. She collapsed into her chair, her sobs echoing through the cave. A woman sitting next to her tucked the two small children into her lap, while another patted the woman's hand.

"We have to do something," a man said. "We cannot allow this evil to flourish. I vote for a bullet to the brain for them both."

Arguments devolved from there, people shouting over one another to be heard.

Manuel's piercing whistle once again brought the room to order. "It's time to vote," he said. "Execution to Ian's side. Abandonment to mine."

While the residents had argued, Manuel and Ian had separated. Everyone except Sophie and Hugh shuffled to cast their vote.

"The community has spoken," said Ian with a nod to Manuel. "Sera and Charles, you will be chained to the wall inside our prison cell, your hands and feet bound, and your mouths gagged."

One man from each side left the residents' ranks and stood behind Sera and Charles.

"You know what to do," said Manuel to the two men. "And bring the keys — every single copy — back to me."

The men walked Sera and Charles out of the room. Murmurs mingled with sighs. But the vote hadn't even been close.

Why did this community shy away from execution for two proven murderers? Was it out of some lingering sense of loyalty? Sophie frowned that the Underground's National Headquarters community seemed to have no backbone. The slight chance of Sera and Charles surviving abandonment was too great a risk for Sophie, but she also refused to go behind their back and against their vote to kill Sera and Charles.

"Now, to address our fate as a community, I invite Sophie up," said Ian. "Sophie is a leader of the Underground in Queenstown and a child of my friends and original Underground members, Matthew and Angie Chen. Please listen and consider her proposal, which I will tell you is our best option."

Sophie stood and joined Ian at the front of the cafeteria. Sometimes she wished she'd known her father, who'd gotten separated from her mother in the chaos of those finals days before Martin conquered Queenstown. She shook her head and focused her attention on the community before her. "First, thank you for your trust. And for the delicious bean soup. Sera and Charles drugged me yesterday, and I hadn't eaten since then."

She licked her lips and looked at her feet. Sophie hated speaking in front of crowds, but Alejandro loved it, relished the eyes on him. So she pulled up every memory of him leading their Underground meetings. She looked up with a smile and relaxed her shoulders down.

"I offer you all the opportunity to join us in Queenstown. Attached to our underground tunnels are several abandoned warehouses. We can house all of you. Your fighters would have meaningful work. The time to confront the Martin regime has come. Martin tried to take us out, but we won't let him have the last word, will we?"

A cheer went up through the crowd, and Sophie deepened her smile. Maybe she could do this public speaking thing, after all.

"The journey will be tough," Manuel said, stepping in front of Ian and Sophie. "We will need to travel in small groups. Some on motorcycles, some in our transports. You'll leave all personal possessions except one small bag each behind. Your bug-out bags are perfect for this. Add whatever food you can fit into your personal bag. But I believe in this community's strength. We have no other option at this point. If we stay, we die. If we head to the IRT, we die. Queenstown is our only option if we want to continue the fight we started forty-five years ago."

The crowd cheered and punched fists in the air.

"All in favor, say 'aye'," said Ian.

The "aye" thundered through the space, echoing back for almost a minute.

"All opposed, say 'nay,'" said Ian.

The silence echoed almost as loudly as the earlier cry.

Sophie locked gazes with the several residents closest to her.

"Alright, let's do this," said Ian, holding his hand high as people moved. "Wait for instructions. You have an hour to prepare. Cooks, please package our last meal and box up our emergency food storage. Take turns to handle your own packing. Teachers, please pack one box of teaching materials, whatever you think we'll need to continue the children's schooling. Medics, please gather your supplies as well. Those assigned to the barns and farm, implement your emergency departure procedure. We will transport pre-selected animals, the supply boxes, and all families with children under five years old in the transport trucks. Everyone else will ride double on motorcycles and the youth and young adults will walk with their group leads. We've planned for this. We all know our jobs. Let's go do them."

The community launched into action, and Sophie marveled at the sight.

"You two should go ahead of us," said Manuel, gesturing to Hugh and Sophie. "Warn your people before we get there. And let's assume all the safe houses are compromised."

"I think that's wise," Hugh said, running a hand through his short curls. "How long do you need?"

"Only a few minutes," said Sophie. "Everything should be within easy reach. We'll need a jerry can of fuel if we aren't stopping at the safe house."

"You got it," said Manuel.

"I'll meet you at the motorcycle barn," said Hugh.

Sophie turned to go, but a hand on her arm stopped her. Ian's eyes crinkled with a smile. "Thank you. Be careful. Alejandro will have my head if you don't make it back safely."

Sophie snorted out a laugh. "He'd have mine, too. Don't worry. We'll be smart. I know what I'm doing, plus I suspect our friend here has some hidden talents." She raised her eyebrows and gestured with her chin toward where Hugh had already disappeared down the storage hallway.

"Crossing the river at Queenstown will be an issue for this many people. The rowboats won't be enough," said Sophie.

"We'll manage," said Manuel. "I know a place."

He knew a place? Could there be an unguarded bridge over the General River or perhaps a boat depot? Had they known of these resources for years only to not use them for lack of an urgent threat?

Sophie shook her head, dismissing the questions. There wasn't enough time to get the answers her mind so desperately craved, and they wouldn't change anything, anyway.

Sophie left the cafeteria, heading toward the female dormitory to find one last person before she fled this nightmare.

After losing one of her best friends, Sophie had realized she needed to treasure her relationships far better. And she'd might as well start with the one in the here and now, although her mind already drifted toward her daughter, Rose.

When Sophie entered the women's dormitory, she crossed to where Candy fastened the buckles on her bug-out bag, the room a cacophony of activity and voices.

"Candy," said Sophie. "I wanted to thank you before I left."

Candy threw her arms around Sophie's neck, and Sophie leaned into the hug, lifting her hands to place them gently on Candy's back. She could do this.

"I can't believe you survived all that!" Candy's voice was loud in Sophie's ear, making her flinch. But instead of startling away from Candy, Sophie buried her face in her friend's warm shoulder.

"I wasn't alone," said Sophie. "Hugh helped." She dropped her arms, but took Candy's hands in her own. "But I couldn't have done it without your warning and insight. You probably saved my life the night they killed Rich."

Sophie used her shoulder to wipe the stray tear escaping down her cheek.

"Oh, Sophie," said Candy, who lifted a hand to stroke Sophie's tangled hair. She'd never gotten that bath, nor would she unless she fell into the General River on the way back to Queenstown. "Of course I would warn you. You're my friend."

"But we never see each other."

"But we're still friends. We've known each other for years," Candy said. "Do you remember that time as teenagers when we snuck onto the radios and talked until dawn?"

Sophie smiled. She sure did. And how long she'd been grounded after her mother had found out. "So worth it. I have to go now, though."

Candy embraced Sophie again. This time, Sophie's touch aversion didn't rear its ugly head.

"Be careful," Sophie said, leaning into the hug.

Candy laughed as she released Sophie. "You're the one who needs to be careful. I'll be with an entire army. See you in a few weeks."

"Do you know how you'll get over the river?"

Candy winked at her. "Top secret information. Only a few of us know, and that never included Sera and Charles."

Sophie hummed. "I don't like that you won't tell me. Once you're safe in Queenstown, if it's okay, I'd love to know. Not out of curiosity, but it's always good to have escape routes."

"Yes, it is. Be safe, my friend."

The two women walked toward Sophie's bunk together, Candy squeezing Sophie's shoulder as she joined her teenaged daughter to help her finish her packing. The young lady stared at Sophie wide-eyed until her mother knocked her shoulder and shook her head.

Sophie finished packing her measly possessions and left the women's dormitory, waving at new acquaintances and others she'd not had the opportunity yet to meet. She'd soon see them again on her turf. Plenty of time to make new friends.

12

Sophie honestly didn't mind the driving rain. It kept the guards in their cozy, heated shack on the lone bridge over the General River. Their crossing lay to Queenstown's west, downriver from the bridge and the patrols who manned the area.

She ducked her head further into her hood and hunched her shoulders, digging the oars into the current. Even if they didn't fall into the swift river, she and Hugh would be soaked by the time they made it across. Sophie had wanted a bath, but not like this.

On their way to the mountains, Rich had stashed their boat far into the woods, beyond the wide levee on the river's south side which kept the General in its banks during heavy spring rains. That the Martin regime maintained the levee and the bridge shouldn't have surprised her, given the river's importance. But with the state of Queenstown's disrepair, it made her wonder at the regime's priorities.

Why did the regime need a paved road heading south? No settlement or military base existed that way. Radiation from the nuclear bombs which had decimated the major cities throughout the southern region of the former USA still contaminated the land, making it uninhabitable even decades later. Clean water sources abounded in the mountains, but not to the east or south of Queenstown.

Or so she'd been told.

Add this to the lies she'd been told.

Sophie scoffed.

"What?" said Hugh. "Do you see something?"

"No, just wondering why we can't spread out beyond the city walls. What a stupid thought. Of course we can't. Martin's control over us would weaken."

"You're just now realizing this?"

"No," said Sophie. She dug deeper with a grunt. The swift current was dragging them too far downriver. They'd have to hike for hours to find the old safe house if they didn't course-correct quickly. "It's just... living every day under his regime, you get used to it. Sometimes I wonder why we're rebelling, why we bother. But then I look at how the kids are growing up, with no idea of the wonders beyond their area's walls, their day-to-day lives dictated by an octogenarian with a serious control streak. I wonder if the regime has even tested the land for nuclear contamination or if they assume it's still uninhabitable."

"I doubt they'd bother," said Hugh. "Nuclear fallout takes decades to work its way out of the ground water. It's a miracle the native vegetation has recovered as well as it has. But growing crops? Nah, not yet. Only in areas the fallout didn't effect, like where you Underground people lived."

"Maybe you're right," said Sophie.

He sounded sure of his opinion. Meaning Great Britain had probably snuck in and tested.

"Here we are," Hugh said, after long minutes of both of them working hard at the oars.

The boat bumped the shoreline, the taller trees up-slope hidden by a dense fog. Sophie had intentionally timed their arrival for nighttime. A dark river crossing was a successful crossing.

Sophie jumped out and hauled the metal boat up the bank, her boots sinking into the mud. Hugh pushed from behind, his feet and legs fully submerged in river water.

"Walls' balls, you're going to stink tonight."

"The river isn't that bad," said Hugh. "Besides, you need a boost with this current and how heavy I am."

It had only been a little over a week since she and Rich had crossed the river heading in the other direction, but it felt like months, given everything that had happened. She still missed her friend — his easy laugh, his willingness to go along with her schemes. And Sophie didn't know how she was going to tell the others. They'd be heartbroken. And incensed.

Hugh and Sophie team-lifted the boat, transporting it up and over the wide levee. They worked through the brush and undergrowth along the old levee, walking past weather-beaten homes and buildings. Abandoned cars littered the streets, but Sophie and Hugh stayed in the shadows, picking their way through backyards and fields until, an hour later, they reached a dark home on stilts.

She and Rich had avoided using this old safe house on purpose, in case they'd been trailed. Good thing Sophie knew how to get inside every safe house along their route, including this one. It was their standard operating procedure before they left the Queenstown Underground facility.

Sophie had to assume the other safe houses concealed a trap. They set the metal boat down, and Sophie dug in the rock garden at the back of the house, searching for where they kept the keys. Her fingers closed around an waterproof box buried under several rock layers and she breathed out a sigh.

Rich had assured her their Queenstown Underground leaders were the only ones who knew about this safe house, but after everything that had happened in the mountains, Sophie had feared patrols would be waiting here for them. And all because Sera and Charles had brought in a regime informant, Joe. Sophie would be angry at their former leaders for a very long time. But she refused to allow their deception and treachery to set the Underground back. No, this had to be the impetus that propelled them into action.

She ran up the back stairs, her revolver in the low-ready position, and unlocked the door on the patio. She cleared the home, then opened the interior door down into the built-in storage area at the bottom level.

Hugh was outside the massive swinging door and together they lifted the metal boat, Sophie gritting her teeth against the racket the boat made when it hit other items hanging inside the storage area. They lowered the door back into place and locked it from the inside.

"Alright," said Sophie. She wiped her forehead and dropped her hood. "Let's go get dry. No lights."

"Of course," said Hugh. "And let's try for silence from here onward. I don't want to find out what the Martin regime will do if they catch me."

"It would be bad."

They tiptoed up the wood stairs and entered the kitchen area, cleared of anything useful decades ago. The two-story home overlooking the river must've been a mansion in the pre-civil war days, the views alone worth a fortune. Now it stood abandoned, its paint all but gone, cobwebs and dust its only inhabitants. They'd passed home after home in similar shape on their journey through nuclear-tainted land. The scale of the former USA still amazed and baffled Sophie. All those people. Gone.

Sophie waved her arms to clear the cobwebs as she walked into the living room. "I'm not sleeping on that." She pointed to a sagging couch, a deeper shadow in the dark room. With the heavy rain outside, she could hardly see the walls to avoid them.

"Floor for me, too."

"Want dinner?"

"Do I want dinner? Of course, I do. I'm a growing boy."

"You are not still growing," Sophie chuckled. "A boy? Maybe."

Hugh punched her in the arm. "Tell me about your daughter. You never talk about her. It's Rose, right?"

Sophie looked up at the ceiling, then grabbed two wrapped sandwiches out of her backpack, passing one to Hugh. Other than a few apples, which they would eat for breakfast, it was the last of their food.

"You're too old for her," she said, pointing at Hugh, who grinned and waggled his head in reply. Her nostrils flared.

"Rose is a genius, but doesn't know her own worth. Before I left Queenstown, she was accepted into Martin's new physicist doctorate program. But this isn't the program at the University of Martinsburg. Her program trains nuclear and astro physicists. Which makes me wary. The international community still forbids Martin from having nuclear weapons or ballistic missiles, right?"

Hugh nodded, his mouth full of the homemade goat-milk cheese sandwich. She'd never tasted anything like it inside Queenstown — and probably wouldn't until they defeated Martin someday far in the future. Hugh gestured for her to continue, which she did after swallowing her too-big bite.

"So, why does he need nuclear physicists? Astro physicists I guess I could see, maybe for a satellite which another nation would launch on top of their rocket. But nuclear? And Rose was dead-set on applying for it. I knew she'd get it. She didn't think I noticed all the college and masters-level textbooks, but how could I not? I don't even know what Matrix Algebra is, but I know it's not offered at the high school."

"I guess it wouldn't be," said Hugh. "Is she still in Queenstown?"

"I hope so," Sophie said. "I have a lot to say to her. Some she'll love to hear. And maybe some things she won't like so much. But they need to be said."

"If she's anything like you, she might be a touch stubborn."

Sophie snorted out a laugh.

Beams of light pierced the dark room, throwing shadows onto the walls. Sophie and Hugh both flattened themselves to the floor. The rain pounding on the roof was the only sound.

Hugh tapped her hand and Sophie's brain quickly caught up to his Morse code communication. "Patrols," Hugh tapped.

"Never," tapped Sophie back.

"Weapons," tapped Hugh, drawing his revolver and army crawling toward the front door.

Sophie drew her weapon and shuffled through the kitchen to the back door, waiting for the footsteps on the stairs outside that would spell their death. Or worse, their capture.

She counted slowly, marking minute after minute. Voices outside filtered through to her and she strained to listen. But it was no use. She couldn't make out anything they said through the downpour. Eventually, the faint voices faded entirely and the rain outside slowed.

She raised onto her knees and crawled to the window.

Nothing.

Sophie tiptoed back into the living room, approaching the door from the other side.

"Anything?" her voice barely registered to her own ears.

"They're leaving," said Hugh, who now stood beside the window, his body in shadow.

"Let's get a few hours of sleep then head out early," Sophie said. "If they're patrolling out this far from Queenstown, we'll need to move in the dark." She couldn't shake the unease at seeing Queenstown patrols this far outside the city. As far as she knew, it had never happened before. Or perhaps Rich hadn't wanted to mention it?

"Agreed. You take first sleep shift," said Hugh. "I'm too keyed-up."

"Why come here? Why does Great Britain care about us?" Sophie clamped her hand over her mouth, hardly believing she'd actually asked Hugh. The young man was a skilled operative of another nation, someone to be respected, not befriended.

Sophie removed her hoodie and her shoes, laying them out to dry. She refused to remove her pants or shirt with Hugh in the same room. If they'd been able to relax in separate bedrooms, maybe she might've been comfortable enough. Plus, they needed to be ready to go at a moment's notice.

"It's complicated," said Hugh, his eyes on the scene outside. The room brightened ever so slightly, making Sophie think the clouds were clearing.

"Explain," said Sophie. "We have all night."

"It won't take that long," said Hugh. "But my nation thinks now is the time to take Martin down. He's vulnerable. Old. His cabinet fights and jockeys for power with each other. Then when he announced this program... needless to say, it raised suspicions in my government."

"Same."

"And that's all I can say."

"Or else you'd have to kill me," Sophie said, wrapping her arms around her torso with a shiver. Being wet was overrated. At least she was mostly clean now. "I get it."

And she really did. If Martin developed or bought nuclear weapons, Sophie knew exactly who he'd go after. And why. The refugees living in the IRT and the Protected Region of Minnesota infuriated him. They were citizens of the FRA in another nation.

Outside of his control. But he'd probably also be insane enough to go after the biggest world powers left — Great Britain, Canada, Mexico, and their allies around the world.

Which was why Rose wanting to join that program ticked Sophie off so much. But she didn't dare tell her daughter the real reason. If Rose knew the full truth, she'd never talk to her mother again. And Sophie simply couldn't bear that possibility. But how much truth was enough for Rose to think she knew everything? That was the million Martin question.

13

Sophie halted behind the abandoned office building, the sight before her stunning her into silence.

"Why are there sentries outside an abandoned warehouse?" Hugh asked, leaning over Sophie to look around the building's corner.

Sophie elbowed him backward and rested her head against the brick facade. "I don't know. They're not patrols, that's for sure. Clothing is way too ragged. Before I left everything was totally normal. Well, except Rose getting accepted into the physicist program and me missing out on that announcement."

She squeezed her ponytail out, flinging the water to the ground. The rain had started again the moment they'd left the old safe house. And it hadn't let up the entire time they'd traveled through the destroyed city, dodging patrols which never used to be there and hiding out in bombed-out, crumbling buildings during the daytime. Every inch of Sophie was wet and aching and all she wanted was a hot shower and a bed. Not necessarily in that order.

Sophie peered around the corner again and smiled at the familiar form now standing outside the supposedly secret back entrance into HQ — Alejandro.

"Let's go introduce you," she said, exiting the shadow of the office building and striding down the middle of the street.

Hugh grabbed for her, but she slipped from his grasp, waving for him to follow her.

The sentries on duty alerted to her presence and lifted their weapons.

Sophie halted in her tracks and whistled the two note safe messenger signal.

Alejandro whistled back, then sprinted for her. Wrapping her into his muscular arms, Alejandro lifted Sophie into the air and spun her, their laughter mingling. Sophie had never been so relieved to see the big lug in her life.

"Where's Rich?" Alejandro asked, looking past her to take in Hugh. She watched as he cataloged every weapon on Hugh and could almost hear him calculating if he could take the British operative down or not.

Sophie pushed out of his embrace, but Alejandro wrapped her in a side hug. "Stop being a jealous old man, Alejandro, and listen to me. This is Hugh McIver, the ambassador from Great Britain to the Underground," Sophie said, patting his chest and her other gripping his forearm, the one which still itched toward his holstered revolver. "Alejandro, Rich is dead."

"What?" Tío's face went slack.

Sophie squeezed his arm hard, forcing his gaze to connect with hers. "Charles and Sera are traitors. They were working with Martin. One of his goons came to headquarters, claiming to have escaped some labor camp outside Martinsburg. Alejandro, there was so much division. It made me so mad and sad all at the same time. When Rich and I probed into what was going on, this guy Joe murdered Rich. I tracked Sera and Charles to where they just dumped his body into a ravine. Then they drugged me—"

Alejandro grabbed Sophie into a tight embrace. "I knew you shouldn't have gone."

She pushed herself back. "Stop. I'm not done yet. They kidnapped me and were going to murder me, but Hugh took out Joe and freed me. Then we returned to the cave and freed Mani and Ian. Sera and Charles had also taken them captive and were planning to kill them, too. Sera and Charles had conspired with the Martin regime to take out the entire population there. Killed in their beds by Martin's bombs if they stayed, ambushed on the journey to the IRT if they fled. No win situation."

"Sophie left out how she had almost freed herself by the time I arrived," said Hugh. "Your gal is a bad ass, Alejandro. But the Underground is in trouble."

"You can say that again," said Sophie, stepping fully out of Alejandro's arms. "The community voted to come here. The saltpeter cave is compromised, as are all our safe houses. Now Queenstown patrols are venturing far beyond the city walls. We had to dodge multiple patrols north of the river on our way here."

"Walls' balls," said Alejandro.

"We knew we needed sentries, but maybe we should also be sending patrols of our own out. Like scouts."

"Agreed," said Hugh. "I can help with that."

A warm body plowed into Sophie. Havana's coconut-scented body products filled her senses, making Sophie smile in recognition. She turned into Abuela's embrace and squeezed her older friend.

Wow, she'd missed this. How long had Sophie gone without a hug or physical touch when she'd been so busy as Peter Kim's assistant and spy? That was a thought she'd need to examine later.

"Juli," said Sophie. "We have news."

"So do we," Abuela, or Juli, as her close friends called her, said. "Let's get out of the rain."

The downpour had slowed to a drizzle, and Sophie hadn't even noticed.

Hugh and Alejandro talked about the patrols behind her as she entered what had typically been an abandoned, dusty warehouse. The signs of occupancy were everywhere. Pallets on the floor, long tables set with chairs to serve dinner, a makeshift kitchen in one end, and a space where kids ran and played.

"What happened? Why are all these people here?"

"There was a labor camp outside Queenstown," said Abuela. "Actually there were three. These are the prisoners from one of them. Marcos, a Havana teen whom Alejandro was supposed to recruit — but he hesitated and I could shoot my son — ended up in one after escaping over the wall. Loco. But Marcos being taken prisoner prompted action on our end and now that camp is freed."

"So it's true. Martin kept the labor camps. We thought Joe lied about that." Sophie couldn't stop examining the camp's former residents. Most wore tattered clothing and were barefoot. "How are we keeping all these people fed? And how will we get clothes for them? Winter is over, and maybe some can make do with what they have over the summer. But we're going to have naked kids if we don't find some clothing fast."

Abuela chuckled. "You're not wrong. Truth is, we're struggling. We've pulled on all the resources we can. I think it's time to bring in the city council, but Alejandro is opposed. Maybe you could sway him?"

Sophie almost rolled her eyes; but that would be far too immature. Still, she wanted to smack some sense into Alejandro. "Of course, he is. I'll work on him."

"If anyone can get him to budge, it's you, Sophie." Abuela gave Sophie a tight side hug as they walked toward the entrance into the Underground, which stood open.

Sophie shook her head at the sight. She never thought Queenstown's HQ would be so stuffed — or so out in the open. She'd spent the last thirty years of her life guarding this secret and to have so many people in the know made her eyelids twitch.

They descended the wooden stairs, the entire staircase shaking with their weight. Someone needed to replace this old thing.

When they reached the bottom, Sophie waited for Alejandro and Hugh to catch up. She linked her arm through Alejandro's and leaned into him.

"How's Rose doing?" she asked.

Alejandro stiffened and turned to face her, gripping her forearms.

Sophie clenched her teeth at his expression.

Abuela froze beside her and Sophie looked from one to the other.

"What is it? Just tell me."

"Soph, Rose is missing," said Alejandro. "She was under house arrest, and Chul was with her. Someone knocked out all the Little Asian patrolmen in the building and nabbed her. Chul said they had documents. Official-looking. He couldn't do anything about it."

Her heart stuttered. Rose was gone? Kidnapped? Arrested?

Sophie collapsed to the ground, Alejandro catching her.

A keening filled the tunnel.

Would anything in Sophie's world ever be right again?

THE END

***

Continue Sophie's and Rose's story in
Caged, Book Two in the *Divided* series
Coming Summer 2025

Also by CC Robinson

Upheaval: A Post-Apocalyptic Prequel to the Divided series

An impossible choice - survive to live in bondage or die.
Available at most major retailers
or to new subscribers to CC's monthly e-newsletter, the Underground
https://ccrobinsonauthor.com

———

Divided: Book One in the Divided Young Adult Dystopian Series
Beyond the walls lies freedom. Beyond freedom lies death.
Four teenagers must choose what price they're willing to pay.
Experience the thrilling first book in the *Divided* series, an
award-winning YA dystopian tale
that will keep you on the edge of your seat and up late at night.
Available at most major retailers

———

Deception, a Divided novella, Book 1.5 in the Divided series
Can Sophie save the Underground and escape with her life,
or will her secrets be buried in the mountains forever?

Available at most major retailers
or to advance reader team members via
CC's Underground newsletter at
https://ccrobinsonauthor.com/divided-newsletter-signup

A Note About Caves

Almost a decade ago I went, mostly willingly, on a trip with my husband's extended family to the hollers of eastern Kentucky — their family origin location. We explored Rock Castle County, KY, drank water from the spring in Climax (have you drunk the water? It's actually delicious), and toured an enormous saltpeter cave. The unique cave system absolutely mesmerized me and I knew I HAD to include this setting in a book. While I was there, I realized this would be the perfect hideout location for a rebellion.

Voilà, we have *Deception*, Sophie's side quest to the Underground National Headquarters inside a cave similar to the Great Saltpetre Cave (spelling of this landmark is according to the website, not conventional American English spelling), but that I made up.

While touring the saltpeter cave, I learned quite a bit:

- The caves were formed through saltpeter mining before and during the War of 1812. Saltpeter is one of three easy-to-find ingredients for gunpowder. Don't try this at home, kids, or you might lose your eyebrows. Many of the miners were impoverished locals, but sadly, many were also enslaved Africans.

- The caves later hosted community gatherings. In the mid-1900s, the Renfro Valley Barn Dance, a bluegrass musical showcase, broadcast from its main Echo Room to a radio station in Cincinnati. The Echo Room (or also called The Maypole or Ball Room) became the inspiration for the cafeteria in *Deception*, though it was always slightly wider and less tall in my imagination.

- The caves' twisting passages open up into smaller "rooms." This reflected the mining process more than anyone's idea of interior design. In this novella the Underground uses these "rooms" as meeting space, dormitories, and family residences. I added size variation to create my fictional living spaces for the Underground's many inhabitants.

- Smoke holes sprinkled throughout the cave system vented dust, smoke, and fire out. This inspired the smoke hole in the kitchen.

- The caves are set deep in the woods, miles away from the nearest interstate (I-75), with a stream and a large clearing. This entire area of the Appalachian foothills is dotted with hills, streams, caves, and woods, making it one of the prettiest places in our nation. Unfortunately, it is also one of the poorest. A careful reading of *Deception* will reveal many of these facets of modern-day Appalachian life and scenery reflected on the pages.

Closed now to visitors except for possibly one day a year, the only way to get inside is through membership in one of a few cave grotto associations. To learn more and see if a public tour is upcoming, visit the Great Saltpetre Cave website at https://gsp.caves.org

Acknowledgements

It takes a village to birth a book out into the world today, and I certainly have one, even for a baby novella!

Thanks to my editors — you know who you are.

Thanks to Raewyn for her help with all things marketing, social media copy, and how to ethically use AI without losing my mind or reputation.

Thanks to my dystopian Facebook group squad — I wouldn't want to write without you all because it would be no fun.

Thanks to my WIP squad for letting me bounce my out-of-left-field marketing ideas off you and for picking apart book descriptions and tag lines. Why can I write an entire book and yet 300 words slay me like an extra in a dragon film?

Thanks to my in-person Cincinnati writing community for your encouragement and cheerleading.

And, as always, thank you to my family and friends who cheer me on even when they have no clue what I do. You're the best! Steve, Ruth, Zach, and Katie Rose, I love you!

And special thanks goes to Grandad for dragging the entire Robinson family, including a load of less-than-willing pre-teens and teenagers, to the old family homestead in rural KY. You are definitely a "mountain doctor" and I'll never forget all your shenanigans during that trip. At least no one got arrested, and we all had a blast! Yes, we drank the water! IYKYK

And last, thank you to you, dear reader. Because without you, I'd write stories that no one would read. And that would be sad.

Speaking of, I love hearing from readers. Reach out on my socials (@ccrobinsonauthor almost everywhere) or on my website. Also, reviews are like warm pancakes with blueberry syrup for breakfast to me. I treasure every review, even the lower stars. Leaving a review on the platform of your choice or wherever you buy books helps other readers find their next keep-them-up-at-night read. Plus, it's valuable feedback for this wee indie author.

About CC Robinson

C C Robinson has over two decades' experience in cross-cultural settings as a medical doctor working in post-civil war nations and as an Associate Pastor at a multi-ethnic congregation led by an African-American man in Cincinnati, the setting for the *Divided* series.

When not donning her superhero cape to save her characters from their own mischief, CC enjoys gardening, hiking, off-roading in her Jeep, and ballroom dancing. She is married to her lifelong best friend, Steve, and they have three grown Gen Z kids, a dog Sadie, and Newt the Cat, who rules the house. She'd love to hear from readers on her socials @ccrobinsonauthor or on her website, https://ccrobinsonau thor.com.